Kira's Quest

Orysia Dawydiak

The Acorn Press
Charlottetown
2015

ACORNPRESS

P.O. Box 22024
Charlottetown, Prince Edward Island
C1A 9J2
acornpresscanada.com

Printed in Canada
Edited by Penelope Jackson
Designed by Matt Reid

Library and Archives Canada Cataloguing in Publication

Dawydiak, Orysia, 1952-, author
Kira's quest / Orysia Dawydiak.

Issued in print and electronic formats.
ISBN 978-1-927502-48-8 (paperback).--ISBN 978-1-927502-49-5 (epub)

I. Title.

PS8607.A968K567 2015   jC813'.6   C2015-904406-5
                                                 C2015-904407-3

Canada Council
for the Arts

Conseil des Arts
du Canada

The publisher acknowledges the support of the Government of Canada
through the Canada Book Fund of the Department of Canadian Heritage
and the Canada Council for the Arts Block Grant Program.

To all my relations, near and distant, who share Kira's spirit of adventure and connection to family.

Chapter One–
The Science of Seafolk

Kira and Cody sat facing the rough waters of Corran Cove, nearly hidden by tussocks of dune grass. They had hunkered down out of the wind and sand for a picnic lunch, propped against the weathered rock sentinels behind them. To an onlooker they would appear to be typical young teens, she with her mane of tousled brown hair, large eyes, and thick glasses, and he a heavyset boy whose teeth gleamed with braces. They unwrapped their salmon sandwiches, uncapped a thermos of hot chocolate, and stared out at the wild waves as they ate.

Cody swallowed a bite and turned to Kira. "So how did your parents figure out your exact birthday, anyway?" he asked, his face serious. "I don't know anyone else born on Hallowe'en."

Kira sipped her hot cocoa and grimaced. "Dad told me he was out fishing on Hallowe'en, the last day of lobster season." She took another bite of her sandwich and chewed. "That's the day he found me. I just popped up right beside the boat!" she laughed. "He was some surprised."

"So were you crying, or what?"

"Not at first. He just scooped me out with the big

net, and as soon as I was out of the water, I changed and started to bawl, and he knew exactly what I was." Kira chuckled. "You know how we feel the cold and heat just like humans when we're not in the sea."

Cody nodded. He remembered his shock two months ago when he first saw Kira transform into a mermaid underwater then change back to human form when she emerged. Since it was novel to her as well, the two conducted a number of tests to learn all the new abilities she possessed as a merrow, the proper term for mermaids and mermen. Compared to humans, her strength and senses under the sea were impressive. Between the experiments Cody had devised and their research on myths and the science of unusual marine life forms, the two had learned a great deal that summer and fall.

"So how old did your dad think you were when he fished you out?"

"They said I looked to be about a year old. Mom decided to make my birthday the same day they found me, because for them it was the day I was born into the family. They couldn't have any babies of their own so I was it."

Cody smiled at her. "Being an only child isn't so bad."

Kira rolled her eyes. "Your parents aren't as strict as mine. I'm under a microscope all the time. I can't get away with anything."

"That's not totally true, not anymore," he pointed out. "Anyway, you know they were trying to protect you from learning who you really were so you wouldn't get hurt in the sea. I mean, the finfolk almost caught you near Hildaland."

Kira pursed her lips and nodded. He was right, of course, but the narrow escape had not diminished her resolve to return to that dangerous island. On an underwater excursion a few weeks earlier, she'd met two merrow cousins who informed her that her real parents, the king and queen of the merrows, were still alive. They told Kira that her parents were prisoners of the finfolk on a mysterious, mist-shrouded island called Hildaland. A place where greedy, treacherous finfolk take their kidnapped human and merrow victims to mine the silver they valued above all else.

Her cousins had convinced her to trust some young finfolk they claimed were friendly to take them to see Hildaland. Kira found the finfolklings creepy, with their sharp features, narrow black eyes, claw-like hands, and green-grey pallor. They had not spoken to her, although they appeared to be on good terms with her cousins. She had one quick glimpse of Hildaland before the finfolklings rushed and tried to grab her. She managed to break free, but couldn't tell if her cousins had been in on the plot to capture her, or if they were caught and imprisoned themselves.

Kira had learned from her dolphin friends that finfolk mostly coexisted with merrows, but they were no friend to humans, dolphins, and other creatures they captured for slaves. Or for food. Since her aunt and uncle had taken over the merrow palace of Merhaven after her own parents were ambushed when she was a baby, it was in their best interest if she, an heir to the merrow throne, was also imprisoned. In fact, her aunt and uncle had probably put her cousins up to the deceit.

"Kira, you're growling!" Cody laughed.

Kira looked up, surprised that she had been so carried away by her thoughts, and noticed for the first time that Cody had dimples. He didn't laugh like that very often. She shook her head and tried to smile.

"I'm going back there someday," she said.

"Yeah, I know. But not until we've done more research and you're prepared. I know you're amazing underwater, but those finfolk are nasty dudes, and you can't do this alone."

Kira shot him a look.

"I mean, you *shouldn't* do this alone. Think how heartbroken your parents would be if you were captured and you couldn't get back. Remember how upset they were when you were missing for one day?" Cody knew he'd never forget the looks of sorrow and guilt on their faces when he confessed to his part in the deception. It was supposed to be a short undersea field trip and Kira had planned to be home before her parents returned from an overnight away. They weren't even angry with him, and blamed themselves for her disappearance—which made him feel especially bad.

Cody stared at the horizon and scratched his chin, in perfect imitation of their science teacher. Mr. Bryson was his favourite teacher and Kira was certain that Cody was not aware of his excellent mimicry. Kira hid her smile; she could tell that her friend was in a serious frame of mind.

"We need to learn more about these finfolk," he finally said. "And how to find Hildaland, and why it never shows up on any maps, or satellite photos, or on Google Earth." He stood up and began to pace, just like his science mentor.

"You told me the dolphins won't go there because it's too dangerous. It's guarded by sharks and finfolk, right?"

Kira stood up and brushed crumbs from her jacket. "Yup, and Cass said they have killer whales patrolling, too. But his dad doesn't know about that because Cass isn't supposed to go anywhere near there," she added. Cass was a young male dolphin Kira had rescued from fishing nets on her underwater expedition. His father, Steen, had repaid her kindness by escorting Kira to

Merhaven, where she had met her creepy aunt, Queen Shree, and her uncle, King Nim, and her treacherous cousins, Borin and Amelie. Pretenders to the throne, Kira thought; traitors to her real parents, the rightful king and queen of the merrow kingdom.

"We've got to dig deeper into the mythology. Maybe your mother knows things she hasn't told you yet. Or maybe Mrs. Doyle can help us find new books. You know, through databases and interlibrary loans."

Kira shook her head. "Mom hates talking about Hildaland. And so does Mrs. Doyle, especially now she thinks her husband is a prisoner there. Mom said they don't know anything more about the place; it was just a story they grew up with."

Bess Cox, Kira's adoptive mother, and Yvette Doyle, the librarian, admitted they were mermaids after Kira returned from her trip to Merhaven. This had shocked Kira more than it did Cody, who immediately listed the physical features all three of them had in common— large eyes, poor vision on land, bigger hands, and wild, curly hair. In fact, Cody's photographic memory and his keen abilities to observe allowed him to identify a number of town residents he believed were changelings—merrows who had chosen to give up the sea and live on land full-time. All of them were married to humans, and most of the couples were childless.

"No way I'm going to ask Mrs. Doyle anything about

Hildaland," Kira continued. "The way she looks at me now, her eyes all teary and her hands shaking, it makes me too sad. And guilty. All we did was find that bottle the seals were playing with."

Cody stopped pacing and flung his arms in the air. "Aha! Babbling Bill!"

"What about him? You think he's a merrow, too?"

"No, but we need to talk to him again. He's the only one we know who says he's seen selkies. He told us where to find the seals, and that's how you found the bottle with Captain Doyle's last message. Before he and his crew were taken by the finfolk , that is. Well, we assume they were finfolk, based on what he wrote and what you saw of them."

"You think old Bill might know about Hildaland?"

"He knows all those old songs and stories. And maybe we should try again to find the selkies, and see if the seals will talk to us." Cody rubbed his hands and began pacing again.

"You mean me. *I* need to find seals who will talk to *me*."

"Yeah, that's what I meant."

"They only barked at me that one time," Kira pouted. "And I think they were afraid of me."

"Maybe we need to find a different group of seals. Maybe Bill can tell us exactly where to find the beach where he saw the selkies dancing around a fire."

"Okay," Kira said. "But right now I need to go home and get ready for Hallowe'en."

They packed up their picnic, carefully gathering sandwich wrappings before they blew away. As they headed down the beach toward town Cody asked, "So, do you celebrate your birthday?"

"Yeah, but not on Hallowe'en. It's no big deal. We always have a cake, but I never liked parties much. Since I dropped out of swimming club, the girls I used to invite over hardly talk to me. But I don't care. I used to go out trick-or-treating with my dad, and Mom stayed home to give out treats. Tonight, I'm giving out the treats."

"Dressing up, maybe? Like a mermaid?" Cody grinned at her.

"Yeah, I joked about doing that, but Mom was not amused." They both giggled at the thought of Bess Cox's stern face amid her riotous red curls.

Then Cody looked at her, serious again. "Do you ever wonder if any people we know might actually be finfolk changed into human form? I mean, they can imitate merrows, so why not humans? Like that crabby clerk at the Quick Stop across from school, she could be finfolk."

Kira laughed. "Oh yeah, she has those mean, squinty eyes, like she's got a trained cobra behind the counter if you give her any trouble. She'd make a great evil witch for Hallowe'en. I'll bet she owns a broomstick."

Cody snickered.

"Except," she reminded him, "when the finfolk came up to the surface, their heads changed into a disgusting slimy cross between a crocodile and a cat. But underwater the rest of their bodies still looked like merrows with dark scales."

"Yeah, but you didn't see them completely out of water. So who knows what the rest of them might turn into," he laughed. "Maybe their bodies turn into gelatinous blobfish, pink slime of the sea world."

Kira shivered. "If the body is anything like the head it's going to be ugly. Sharp and spiky, I'll bet. I hope there aren't any finfolk in town, that's too disturbing to think about. Hallowe'en costumes are bad enough."

They had stopped in front of Kira's small blue clapboard house on the hill above the town wharf. "So, happy birthday, Kira." Cody grinned at her. "And a lucky year, too!"

"Thanks Cody, you're the best," she said, sticking her tongue out at him and pretending to scowl. According to the Cox family calendar, Kira was turning thirteen.

Chapter Two– Selkie Lore

With her house overlooking the wharf and her grand-father's old spyglass in hand, Kira watched for Babbling Bill over the next several days. In all but the worst weather, old Bill, perched on a crate, his fiddle tucked under his bearded chin, could be found entertaining anyone who'd listen. She hadn't seen him in a while, and remembered a conversation her parents had not long ago. The old retired fisherman had caught the flu and landed back in the hospital for a few days. That was two weeks ago.

This Sunday was so still, the afternoon sun glinted off harbour water as flat as the tide pools trapped on high rocky beaches. No action on the wharf, either. Kira scoured the horizon one more time in case a boat, anything, was moving. A final pass over the wharf, and there he was in the middle of her round eyepiece. Babbling Bill limped across the worn grey planks in his tall green rubber boots, fiddle clasped tightly under his arm. He was waving his free arm as if talking to an invisible companion. Kira swept her spyglass up and down the wharf and over the boats tied up to be certain no one else was about. She ran to the telephone and began to dial.

"Cody?"

"Speaking," he answered at the other end.

"Code blue!"

"I'll be there in ten minutes."

"I'm going down now. He doesn't have an audience and we don't want to lose him."

"Good thinking. See you in nine minutes."

Kira heard her mother calling just as she opened the door to leave. "Where are you off to now?"

"I wanted to say hello to Bill down at the wharf." Kira was standing in the doorway, grasping the door handle, when her mother appeared.

"That's nice, Kira. He hasn't been well lately. Why don't you ask him if he'd like to stop by later, maybe have supper with us?"

"Sure, Mom." Kira felt her legs twitching and started to close the door.

"He eats at the boarding house, but I'm not sure how good the food is over there."

"Uh-huh," Kira answered and looked outside.

"You go on now, before he leaves, though the poor fellow can't move fast with his bad leg."

Kira shut the door before her mother said anything more. She was on the wharf in less than two minutes. By then Babbling Bill had set himself down on a lobster trap and was tuning his fiddle.

"Hello, young Kira Cox!" He bellowed out his usual

welcome as she slowed to walk the last few steps.

He had a voice that carried over a great distance, but today it seemed a little wobbly, like old Bill himself. He grinned at her, his eyes squinting beneath white eyebrows that reminded Kira of bristly bottle brushes. Then he winked at her and launched into a lively tune. She recognized the song, an old sea shanty favoured by the fishermen about selkies and other seafolk, though Bill was not singing along this time.

Kira's eyes widened with worry. Did he know her secret, too? What she really was? Her heart began to race and she wondered how many people in the village might know. If Cody could recognize merrows on land, so could all the people who knew about them. She'd asked her mother if there were other merrows besides herself and Mrs. Doyle, but her mother had been vague, saying that there might be one or two here and there up and down the shore.

Cody arrived on the wharf, panting from his run, and sat on a lobster crate next to Kira. He also gave her a wink, then looked up at Bill who was winking at him. What was with all the winking?

Bill finished his tune and the friends clapped. He bowed his head, smiling.

"Thanks, ye're too kind. My voice isn't up to singing today—still creaky from the flu, it seems. I tell ya, I've had enough chicken soup I should be sproutin' feathers any day now. You watch; I'll wake up one morning crowin' at the rising sun. Give me fish chowder any day, that'd suit me just fine. And give me back me voice, ay!" he shouted then started to cough.

Cody and Kira looked at each other, alarmed.

"You all right, Bill?" Cody asked and began to rise.

"All right, all right. Right as rain, bright as sun, don't ye worry, lad," he said. He took a deep breath, coughed once more, shook his head, and laughed. "I'm not dyin' yet, young Cody." He set down his fiddle and bow, then regarded them with a more serious expression, though the corners of his mouth twitched. "Now, while I've been mending, what have you two young folk been up to?"

Kira and Cody looked at each other again. What did Bill know? What had he heard? It was a small town; everyone knew everyone else's business. A young girl disappearing for an entire day was not a typical occurrence and Kira's parents had come up with an explanation that some were likely to question. But most of the buzz was about the bottle that they had found with the message and log notes from Captain Doyle. Very few people knew what he had written, only that he had disappeared ten years ago and that the bottle had probably come from his lost fishing vessel.

Cody began. "Well, um, you probably heard that I found a bottle washed up on a beach, and it belonged to Captain Doyle?"

Bill nodded. "Yes, lad, I did."

"And did you know that there were seals in that cove?"

"There's seals in many of the coves hereabouts."

"I suppose," Cody answered. "But these seals were playing with the bottle. That's how I noticed it." Kira and Cody studied Bill carefully for his reaction.

"Were they, now?"

"Yes. And we were wondering if maybe the seals could be selkies, and maybe they wanted us to have the bottle."

"Oh, was it the two of ya then, watching the seals? I remember ya asking where ya could find 'em."

Kira held her breath for a moment. Cody had told everyone that he found the bottle himself; Kira's parents had forbidden her to be anywhere near the sea. It was she who had seen the seals playing with the bottle underwater, and when they dropped it she brought it back up to the boat where Cody waited for her.

"It's true, seals can get up to a lot of mischief," Bill said without waiting for them to answer his question. "I don't know if they were selkies or wanted ya to have the bottle. For certain they trust children more than grownups, and with good cause," he chuckled. In the summer he'd told them that once, as a young man, he'd seen selkies dancing around a night fire.

Female seals that came on shore shed their skins and danced for joy, revelling in the use of the two legs they were denied beneath the waves. If a human stole the sealskin before a selkie could slip back into it, she could be taken as a wife on land.

Cody continued. "So we wondered if we could find the seals that are selkies, maybe, if you remember where you saw them dancing that one time. And maybe they would talk to us, and tell us if Captain Doyle is still alive, and where he might be."

Bill roared with laughter. "Aha, so that's what ye're after! Well, I never. It's not likely ya'd ever find 'em. People have tried, but I've not heard of any others that've seen 'em these past sixty years or so. I'm thinkin' they've moved on or died off. Or maybe they're all wives on shore now." His shoulders continued to shake with mirth as he picked up his bow and fiddle again.

"But wait," Kira protested, "you said they trust children more. They might trust us, talk to us, if they're still here. Why not?"

Bill moved his bow across the strings, sending out a low, melancholy note like the mournful howl of a dog. He was no longer smiling, his face as long as the sad note. He put down the bow and looked across at them.

"First of all, they have caught on to our human trickery. And did you know, only female seals can be selkies? They've learned to sense when the male members of our kind are around, and they will not leave the water if men are about." He stared at Cody.

"How old are ye, lad? Fourteen, perhaps?"

"Uh, thirteen," Cody replied.

"Too old, then. They wouldn't come anywhere near ya. Now Kira, they might tolerate you, who's to say?"

Kira sat up straight. "How do you know all this?" she asked. Was he playing them, pulling their legs?

Bill set the fiddle on his lap and tugged on his crinkly white beard. "D'ye think I'm makin' this up? Ye know they call me Babblin' Bill, and that I tell stories, some truthful, some fanciful. That's what they say."

Kira stared at Bill but he didn't wink. Six months ago she wouldn't have believed any of Bill's stories. Six months ago she didn't believe in mermaids.

"I believe you," she declared. "I just wanted to know how you learned all this stuff."

Beside her Cody nodded his head.

"Well then, I'll tell ye," he began. "A long time ago, before your parents were born, I knew a man who took a selkie for his wife. He was a fisherman who lived alone in a small house not far from here. At first she enjoyed the adventure of livin' on land and the two of 'em were very happy together. But she began to pine for the sea after a while. She missed seein' her sisters and cousins and other friends she'd left behind.

They had no babies of their own and she spent her days knitting mitts and sweaters for poor and orphan children. Her husband could see she was mourning her old life and family, though she claimed she loved him. So one day he told her she could return to the sea to visit them. And he gave back the sealskin he'd taken from her years before. She didn't know he'd kept it for her all that time."

Bill shook his head and picked up his fiddle. He began to play a soft quiet tune, then resumed his story while he continued to play. "She promised she'd return at the next full moon, and she told him where to wait for her. A few weeks passed before the full moon, and there he was on the beach, hiding in the shadows as he'd been told to do. And what do you suppose happened?"

Kira and Cody looked at each other, eyebrows raised. "She didn't come out?" Cody suggested.

"That's right, lad. A no-show that night. And the next full moon, and the one after that. He fretted that some harm had come to her. He knew seals were sometimes caught in nets by accident and drowned, or killed by sharks, or even by fishermen. Up north they like to make seal-flipper pie, ye know." Bill shuddered and his enthralled audience shivered at the thought.

"He returned to that cove every full moon for a year, hoping she'd reappear. On the thirteenth full moon, which he swore would be the last time he'd come to look for her, there she was, wet and naked and glowin' in the moonlight. He couldn't believe it at first. He just stood there, stunned. But when she saw him, she opened her arms wide and cried out with joy and they came together again."

Bill continued to play, his head down, and Cody and Kira were both relieved he didn't look up right away. They were still blushing at his description of the selkie out of her skin. When Bill raised his head Kira was taken aback at his show of emotion—he'd been crying. That fisherman must have been a very close friend.

"So what happened to her?" Cody asked. "Why did it take her so long to return?"

"Ah, the sea can be an exciting and dangerous place," he said, looking at Kira asquint. "At first she lost track of time. She enjoyed the company of her family so much she nearly forgot she had a husband on land. And here's an interestin' fact: the selkie memory underwater is disconnected from the memory on land. But when they are on land, they remember their seal world only too well. It is the curse of being a landed selkie."

Bill paused to cough, though he continued to play his fiddle, a livelier tune now emerging. "Still, as she had promised, she was on her way back to the meeting spot on that first full moon night when she was caught in a net and pulled up onto a ship. They took her to a place a long way from her husband's village, far, far to the south, and put her into a large salt pool with other seals, some not even the same species as her clan. She later told her husband that some of the pale grey ones were quite nasty, but they'd been captive for most of their lives. Some were even born there in that pool. She despaired of ever returning to her husband, and she almost didn't. But one of the new keepers forgot to latch a sea gate properly and she managed to open it one night and all but the grey seals escaped. So you see, she still had some memory of how latches worked on dry land, or she might still be there. If she lived so long."

"Why didn't the grey seals leave when they had a chance?" Kira asked.

Bill had stopped playing again, and chuckled. "We can only guess, lass. I suppose it was the only life they knew. Leavin' it for the open and unknown sea was more frightening perhaps than living in a place where they were safe from danger. And they'd probably grown lazy and didn't want to hunt for their own food. If Cor—um, the selkie had told 'em stories about life outside their enclosure, they would most certainly have been nervous and perhaps terrified of livin' out there."

Bill snapped up his fiddle and played a fast-paced jig

before either of them could ask any more questions. When he finished he stood up and bowed, while Kira and Cody clapped.

"I must be off again, children, I'm still a bit weak and need me rest." He turned and began to walk slowly down the wharf, Cody and Kira close behind him.

Cody hurried alongside the limping old man. "Um, Bill, is she, the selkie, still alive?"

"Ah, no, she passed away some years ago. But they were happy together until the end, and she never asked to return to the sea."

Kira had more questions, too. "Is her husband still alive?"

"He is, lass, but he's an old, old man."

"But maybe he could tell us more, like where to find the selkies if they're still around."

Bill stopped and faced the two eager faces. "It's nice ye're so keen to see selkies, but he's a brokenhearted old man. He loved his wife dearly, he still mourns her all these years later, and he doesn't want to talk about her or selkies to anyone. Off ye go now, and I'm away, too." With that he wobbled unsteadily up the hill to his boarding house.

"Hmm," Cody mused, "I've never seen him sad like that. And in a hurry to leave."

"I've never seen him cry," Kira said. "Anyway, he's not feeling well, and he is old. We'll just have to go find that cove ourselves."

"Sure, I'll get some maps and we can make a plan. Want to meet after school tomorrow?"

"Okay, see you then."

It wasn't until Kira was inside her house that she remembered her mother's request to ask Bill to supper.

"Mom?"

"Yes, Kira," Bess said as she laid plates on the table.

"Bill wasn't feeling too well so he went back to his place."

"Oh, the poor man. He's been through so much. Can you bring the cutlery, Kira?"

"Sure. Mom, when did Bill's wife die?"

"Oh my, I suppose it was about eighteen, twenty years ago now. Was he talking about her? I know he still misses her terribly."

"What was her name?" Kira asked as she set down the forks.

"Let me think, um, Coralanne, or Coralene, something like that."

"Did she have a job? Did they have any kids?"

"No, no children, and she didn't work outside the home, at least not for money. She was quite the quilter and knitter. She did a lot of charity work, organized shipments of mitts, socks, scarves, and sweaters to orphanages all around the world. She was a kind, generous lady. And she loved her Bill."

"Oh."

Was Babbling Bill confused, mixing up his own life with someone else's? Did he make up the story and pretend his wife was a selkie? Or was he being crafty, telling some truth but holding back the rest? How to tell fact from fancy? That's what Kira took to bed with her that night.

Chapter Three–
Unlikely Conspirator

Kira hoped she could get past Mrs. Doyle without being seen, but that was not to be. Nobody escaped the librarian's attention from her high perch behind a massive desk near the library entrance. Like other merrows, her eyes were large, though her eyesight was bad and she had to wear thick glasses like Kira and Bess.

"Hello, Kira! Anything I can help you with today?" She smiled, peering down at the girl. Kira stopped and stared up at her, surprised at the librarian's cheery tone. Ever since Mrs. Doyle had received the notes written by her husband lost at sea, she had worn a long, grim face. Kira was about to say no, but she changed her mind.

"Umm, maybe you can. I'm looking for more information on selkies. Are there any books you can recommend?"

Mrs. Doyle pursed her lips and for a moment Kira was afraid she'd made a mistake with her request. After all, Mrs. Doyle knew she was already familiar with those library shelves. She and Cody had read nearly every volume on Celtic mythology in the library, and had even ordered books through interlibrary loan. They didn't care that kids at school called them book-worms and bookends and brainiacs.

The librarian leaned over and said in her more usual hushed voice, "Anything in particular you want to know?"

Kira, slightly shocked, realized that this reserved and formal adult was treating her as an equal of sorts, possibly verging on friendship. Yvette Doyle and her mother were close friends, and now she was also being included in that circle of mermaid sisterhood.

"I'd like to talk to a selkie, if I can find one," she blurted, then put her hand over her mouth. Mrs. Doyle straightened up again, all business as she slipped off her stool and motioned for Kira to wait. She walked to an aisle where an assistant was re-shelving books to their proper places. They spoke and Mrs. Doyle pointed at the main desk. The young woman nodded, then walked over and climbed up on the stool.

"Come with me, Kira," Mrs. Doyle instructed, and they walked into her office behind the desk. The librarian closed the door, then said, "Would you like some tea or juice? I have oatmeal cookies here, too, for meetings and consultations." She gave Kira a knowing nod at that last word. "Please sit if you like," she said, waving at a chair. "I'm having tea. Would you like some?"

"Um, okay, tea would be fine."

While she turned on the kettle to heat water and got out the cups and a plate of cookies, Yvette Doyle asked Kira about school. What did she like the most, the least? How was her friend, Cody? And by the way, she told Kira, Cody had been in the library earlier that day, studying sea charts and nearby coastline contours. A very smart young man, in her opinion.

Once they were settled with their tea, Mrs. Doyle said, "So, you'd like to meet a selkie and talk to her, would you?"

"Um, yeah. Do you think selkies are real, Mrs. Doyle?" For the time being she decided not to say anything about Babbling Bill's stories.

"To be honest, dear, I've never had the occasion to see one on land, but we heard a lot about them when I was young and still living undersea. What I do know is that they are a little shy around anything larger than they are, including merrows. There are a number of creatures that can change undersea and imperson-ate other beings. Some can even camouflage them-selves and become nearly invisible. Seals are wise to be wary," she said, sipping her tea. "As you probably know, some people like to eat seal meat, and a lot of fishermen hate seals because they compete with humans for fish."

"I heard they won't come out of the water if there are men nearby," Kira said. "And they may not trust any adults, only children. Is that true?"

"Correct on both counts. And also, they will only emerge at night and on a full moon. For some reason that is the only time they can shed their skins and express their human features." She nibbled on a cookie and grinned at Kira. "And you probably know that not all merrows can change back and forth between human and merrow forms, depending on their age."

Kira nodded. Her mother had shared that last bit of merrow lore when Kira wanted to know why her mother never went into the water. She worried that this might happen to her, that someday she would lose her ability to change back into a mermaid. Not until full adulthood, she'd been assured, though no one could say exactly when that might be.

As they sipped their tea and chewed on oatmeal pecan cookies, one of Kira's favourites, she decided to confide further in Yvette Doyle, and hoped it would not upset her. "You know, I was the one who found the bottle. I was underwater when I first saw it."

A shadow seemed to darken the librarian's watery blue eyes for a moment before they cleared again. Her smile was weak but she nodded. "I rather thought that was the case, dear. I knew all along you were one of us, of course."

"I noticed the bottle because seals were playing with it. They dropped it when they saw me. I tried to talk to them but they seemed frightened and swam off right away."

"I expect they haven't seen merrows in these waters for some time. They were probably suspicious of who or what you really were."

"But maybe they wanted us to have the bottle? Maybe they knew a human had put the bottle in the water with a note?"

Yvette Doyle sighed deeply and shook her head. "Oh, my dear, seals have no reason to help people. They consider most humans to be enemies. In general seals and selkies have no quarrels with merrows, but finfolk are another matter. Those despicable creatures can morph into very good copies of merrows and give us a bad name."

Kira remembered the drawings of finfolk in the books she and Cody had studied. Some had spiky fins projecting from their heads and backs, clawed hands, and faces similar to humans. There were also finfolk who took on merrow features, though their eyes were never as large. Kira had a sudden vision of her aunt, Queen Shree—those small, darting eyes, the black, snaky coils of hair, the yellowed hands with claw-like fingernails. Of course she had to be finfolk! That was why the finfolklings who had accompanied Kira and her two cousins to Hildaland looked so familiar. Ugh! Her uncle, King Nim, looked like a regular merrow, and her mother Bess said that he could well be a half-brother to Kira's father, as he had claimed. But that meant her sneaky cousins were half finfolk, and she had trusted them!

Now that they had gone this far, Kira wondered if she dared push on and broach the unmentionable. She thought of the Harry Potter books, and how everyone feared to speak the evil Voldemort's name. Could she speak of Hildaland, the place that "shall not be named," to a woman whose husband might be a prisoner there—along with her own royal parents?

She swallowed. "Mrs. Doyle, you may not want to talk about this, but do you think my parents and your husband could be on Hildaland?"

A small sob escaped from the librarian, who had now dropped her eyes and covered her mouth. Suddenly her hand shot out and grasped Kira's across the table. "Yes!" she nearly shouted, her chin quivering. "Yes, it is very possible. And you saw the place with your own eyes, didn't you?"

Kira nodded, afraid to speak. A current of fiery emotion flowed into her arm and through her body. Her eyes began to burn. When Mrs. Doyle let go, Kira gasped for air.

Kira whispered, "I need to go back there, somehow. The dolphins won't go, and I don't blame them. I want to talk to the seals, to the selkies. Maybe they're afraid of it, too, but maybe they can tell me how to find it."

Again Yvette Doyle shook her head. "If you could find a selkie who'd talk to you, which is highly unlikely by the way, you couldn't possibly go on your own. You wouldn't, would you?" Her eyes widened with concern.

"No, of course not. I just want directions so we can figure out a way to get there. That's all. I want to find my real parents."

Mrs. Doyle's eyebrows shot up.

"You know what I mean. I love my parents here, they *are* my parents, they saved me, took care of me and everything. I just can't stand the thought of all those people who've been captured, and maybe they're slaves, and being mistreated, and..." She trailed off as the face across from her blanched.

"We have to do *something*, don't we?" Kira eventually said. "We should at least *try* to find them."

Yvette Doyle was patting Kira's hands, crying silently. "Yes, dear, we have to try. But you mustn't put your own life in danger. If I help you, and you then run off and any harm comes to you, Bess—the mother who raised you, my best friend in the world—will never forgive me. And I will never forgive myself. We have already lost so much. Do you understand?"

Kira gulped. "Yes, I understand. So you'll help me?"

Mrs. Doyle covered her wet eyes with her large

merrow hands. "You're right, dear. We have to try."

Kira sighed and leaned forward. "You know Babbling Bill? He told Cody and me a story about someone who took a selkie wife a long time ago. We wanted to know where that fisherman found her, but Bill says that she died and her husband doesn't want to talk about her."

The librarian's hands slid to the tabletop and she gave Kira a weak smile. "Leave that piece of the puzzle with me. I think I know how to find out. My training in library science and research comes in handy at times like this." She stood up and Kira followed. "Are you going to tell Cody what we're up to?"

Kira suddenly had doubts. She knew Cody would do anything to help her in this quest, but she was starting to feel guilty about dragging him into another escapade that might get him in trouble again. "Do you mind?"

"It's up to you."

By the time she'd stepped outside, Kira had decided to share what she had learned from Mrs. Doyle. If there was going to be trouble, she wanted Cody on her side. And she knew he'd be deeply hurt if she left him out of her plans. Anyway, now there would be two of them if anything should happen to her, which it wouldn't. She hoped.

Yvette Doyle was indeed an astute and diligent researcher. She didn't reveal the source of her information, but she was confident that *if* there were going to be any selkies emerging from nearby waters, she knew the exact place. Over and over she cautioned Kira not to get her hopes too high, that the odds were against ever seeing any selkies.

She continued to repeat this as they quietly rolled out of town at 11:30 p.m. one night in mid-November. Kira had slipped out of the house when her parents were asleep. She could count on their pattern of early to bed, early to rise, and a deep, sound sleep in between. Yvette Doyle drove them south along a coastal road that wound through mostly uninhabited scrubland filled with large grey boulders and stunted evergreens. The moon was rising, the night was clear and cold. Between rock outcroppings and tree branches they could spot the moon reflecting off the water. After half an hour, Mrs. Doyle turned off the main road onto a nearly hidden dirt track and down into the trees. She parked the car, exhaled loudly and regarded Kira.

"Are you sure you want to go through with this?"

"Yes!" Kira said, and launched herself out of the car in case Mrs. Doyle changed *her* mind.

With the help of a powerful flashlight, they found an overgrown path and began pushing through. The reassuring sound of waves lapping the shore grew steadily louder until they squeezed between two towering stones and emerged onto a small, pebbly beach.

Yvette Doyle turned off her flashlight. Powerful moonlight flooded the area, revealing huge boulders that reached far into the water on each side. They were cut off from the beaches to the north and south, inside a perfect C shape opening out to the Atlantic Ocean.

"How in the world would anyone ever find this place, especially at night?" the librarian mused. She had already visited the beach in daylight to make sure she knew where to go in the dark. "There must be magic here, something that draws seals and humans together. As for myself, I find it creepy and I want to take you straight home, Kira. I can't leave you here alone! What was I thinking? What would your parents say?"

"No, Mrs. Doyle! Don't think like that. You won't be far away, and I'll use the cell phone you gave me if there's a problem. I'll just sit quietly in this shadow between these two giant rocks." Kira snuggled between two weathered sentinels and tucked in her booted feet. "No one can see I'm here. Can you see me?"

"Of course I can't see you, child, my night vision is terrible, as you know." She paused, and they both listened to the waves. The sound was hypnotic, relaxing. Kira closed her eyes and laid her head against a boulder.

"Very well, I'll leave. But I'll only be half a kilometre down the road where I showed you, and I'll be listening. I'll be back at four in the morning, sharp. But if you want to leave earlier you call me on the cell. And you know where to find the car, right? And you have your flashlight?"

"Yes, Mrs. Doyle. Don't worry."

Yvette Doyle leaned down and rested her hand on Kira's head for a long moment before turning and walking back up the invisible path to the car.

Kira was so worried she might fall asleep and miss the selkies, it never occurred to her to be afraid, alone in the dark. In fact she had never felt so alert before. Every nerve in her body was singing, like the current from Mrs. Doyle's hand to hers, but milder, almost pleasant. The feeling was familiar and she tried to remember why.

Kira closed her eyes and tried to imagine what she was doing, where she was when she felt that warm tingling before. She pictured her mother, Bess agitated, happy, or upset—anytime she was in a strong mood and touched Kira. That's when Kira would feel the peculiar sensation. The last time she'd felt that electric surge was the night she returned home from her undersea field trip. Her parents had feared she was lost forever, and she'd been desperate to return home after escaping the finfolk ambush. Her father, Cillian, loved Kira just as much, if not more, but his hugs did not evoke the same sensory response as her mother's touch. Was this a mermaid thing, she wondered?

Whatever it was, chemistry or electrical energy or magic, Kira was certain something would happen tonight. The very air in this little cove with no official name was alive.

Chapter Four–
Selkie Magic

"Shush. It's a human girl-child."

"More like a middling, I'd say."

"D'ye think she ran away? Why's she alone?"

"We should be careful, she might be bait."

"But no one's come in dozens of moons, why now?"

"There's no one else here but her. I sniffed all around."

"Someone else was here earlier. I can tell."

"Shall we wake her?"

"Not yet. She'll awake when she smells the smoke, like as not." Giggles and rustles as the figures scurried off into the nearby brush.

Kira cracked her eyes open, but there was nothing to see except for the beach in front of her, the waves and the heavy moon illuminating the scene. Did she just dream those voices? She strained to listen. Twigs snapped, more giggling in the bushes. She was not alone—they had come after all!

She watched as the women, five in all, emerged from between the boulders carrying bundles of kindling. They moved in unison, like a team of synchronized swimmers, dropping the twigs then weaving them into a wreath. They leaned over, their heads meeting in the middle of a circle, and they began chant. Kira could not make out words but the sounds were rhythmic and soothing.

Then a flame leapt out from the middle as their heads snapped back and they all rose, hands clasped together. They skipped, they dipped, they flowed around and around the fire, never stopping. Their bodies rose and fell, first one then the other. The bobbing reminded Kira of games she and her school friends played when they were very young. But these figures were those of mature women, and, yes, they were naked. For some reason that fact did not bother Kira. She scanned the beach and saw what might be piles of their sealskins near the water's edge. She didn't remember those mounds being there when she and Mrs. Doyle first arrived.

Eventually the women broke their circle. First one left, twirling toward the water, then another. Kira suddenly felt panic. What if they left and she never spoke to them? But before she stepped out of her shadowy corner, one of the women, an older one, ran toward her.

"Have you wakened, girl-child?" she called out, stopping a few feet away.

Now Kira felt so self-conscious she couldn't speak. She stood up and stepped away from the boulders.

Another selkie joined the first one. "Have you been spying on us, small human?"

"Uh, yeah, I guess so. I came here to meet you. I'd like to talk with you." Kira cleared her throat and the selkies jumped back. "I'm sorry, I don't mean to frighten you. I wanted to ask for your help. To find my parents."

The selkies by the water had returned and all five gathered in front of Kira, eyeing her like she was the most curious thing they had ever seen.

"Our help?" the elder selkie said. "You humans are odd. Come sit by the fire with us and explain yourself. Speak slowly and be clear. We are not here for long."

Kira followed them to the fire and sat on the rough, pebbly ground. The five women sat in a semi-circle across from the fire. Kira explained her quest, that she had seen Hildaland herself by accident but wished to learn how to return there. She had brought pencil and paper and was prepared to write down directions and to sketch a map if they could give her enough details and landmarks.

"A map?" The selkies giggled and shook their heads.

"We cannot help you with a map. We can tell you what things to look for underwater, but we do not measure distance the way you do. We use time, but that changes with currents and how fast we swim."

"But I'll be sailing there in a boat. Or maybe with several boats, so we need to know what to look for on shore."

Again the selkies giggled, except the oldest one, who stood up. "And why should we help you? You humans hunt us, trap us, take us from our homes, let us drown in your nets. Why should we do anything for you? You are a stranger, you are not kin."

"Well, I'm not a human, either!" Kira retorted, then wished she hadn't. The other four selkies jumped to their feet, then crouched as if ready to run for the water.

Kira rose slowly. "Wait, I'm a mermaid, that's what I meant. I won't harm you, I'm here alone." Kira crossed her fingers behind her back, praying they didn't catch her in the partial lie.

The older selkie approached, eyeing Kira with suspicion. "How did you find this place?"

Kira was about to clear her throat again, but stopped herself. She supposed it might sound like a growl to the selkies. "Well, there is this old fisherman, we call him Babbling Bill—"

"Bill?" The selkies surged toward Kira, excited.

"Yes, Bill. He was telling me a story about a friend who had a selkie wife—"

"What was her name?" the old selkie barked out.

"Uh, I'm not sure. But Bill's wife was something like Cora, Coralanne—"

"Coralene!" they shouted in unison.

"Okay, Coralene." Kira was uncertain if this was a good or a bad thing, or if his wife really was Coralene.

She waited, nervous.

"Sit!" the elder commanded all of them, and they obeyed, once again facing each other across the fire. The flame continued to blaze evenly without additional fuel, as if it was burning of its own accord.

The elder appeared to be glaring at Kira, her dark eyes deep, bottomless pools. "Is Coralene alive?" she asked in a quiet voice.

"My mother said she died about twenty years ago."

The selkies murmured but did not show any emotions.

"Yes, we heard this, but did not know if it was true," the elder said. "She was my sister. I am called Solina."

Kira gasped. "Oh, I'm sorry." She was trying to do the math in her head. That would make Solina about eighty years old, or more. She looked much younger than the human eighty-year-olds Kira knew.

"And we are her cousins," said another selkie.

Once more Kira was perplexed. Did this mean they would not help her because someone she knew took their sister away from them? They didn't seem very fond of humans.

"You say you are a merrow. Show us. We may be able to help you."

"Uh, oh, okay." Kira removed her coat, her boots, and her glasses and walked toward the water. The first meeting of skin and icy water made her shiver.

The air was barely above freezing. But one more step and she dove into the waves, immediately feeling as warm as if she'd snuggled into her flannel bed sheets at home. Just as quickly she turned back to make sure the selkies were still on the beach and hadn't tricked her by leaving.

She stood up in the shallow water, shivering again in her drenched, human form. The selkies remained where she had left them, but now they were smiling, their bodies relaxed.

"Come to the fire, merrowling. Zolaya, bring her coat, quick!"

Kira crouched close to the fire, rubbing her hands to dry them. The selkies knelt around the other side again, humming and clapping their hands.

Coralene's sister stood up and shook her head as if to clear water from her ears. "We made a decision. We will help you. We have no quarrels with true merrows."

"Th-thank you," Kira said.

"We are angry with Bill for taking Coralene from us, but we know he was kind. And he set her free. She made the choice to return to him. We will do this for Bill, in her memory."

Kira nodded and smiled with appreciation. She didn't trust herself to speak.

"We have little time left in this moon. We cannot help you with a map, but we can take you near to Hildaland.

The finfolk are our enemies, and yours also. There are many dangers at the border, and no human surface craft has ever passed through their barriers. You must go underwater. And you must come with us now."

"Wh-what?"

"It is your choice, merrowling. We cannot leave it to another moon. Our kin will not agree to this if we ask them, which we must do if we return to them first. It is a dangerous journey for us, and especially for you. We can outswim and outsmart the sharks. The orcas are clever but they are not so fast. And our bark can put them off our trail—it pains them." The elder had crossed her arms, her legs planted wide, reminding Kira of her stern gym teacher. "Will you come?"

"Uh, yes, I guess so. Yes!" She tried to push away the pictures of Mrs. Doyle patiently, nervously, waiting in the car, and worse, her parents sleeping in their bed with no inkling of what she was about to do.

"Once we are underwater, we are natural seals and we cannot speak to you, nor you to us. If we meet danger, we will push you toward the shore where you should be safe. When we can, we will come for you. Understood?"

"Yes." Kira's mind was racing. She had a million questions, but she couldn't think of one under all that pressure.

She didn't have to. Solina continued. "As we near the

border, you will feel a strong current, a whirlwater, swirling up to the surface then down again, around and around. We will go no further. You can proceed if you wish, but there is no guarantee you will survive the trip to that evil island. Every animal you see is a potential enemy, so hide if you spot anything half your size or larger. You may run into patrolling sharks and orcas, and there may be giant squid. We have seen them over three times your size on this side of the border; who knows what monsters lurk on the other side. Closer to the island I imagine there will be finfolk guards as well, and they can shift into nearly any shape they wish. Be suspicious of everything! None of us know what you will find on the island. No living creature has ever returned to tell us."

"The moon is low," one of the selkies warned.

"We must leave now. Will you come?" The elder selkie's eyes were serious, but there was a smile on her lips.

"Y-yes. But I need to leave a note. For another merrow who brought me here. She'll be back at daylight and I promised I would wait. I need to let her know where I'm going."

"No time, merrowling!"

But Kira had already removed the notepad from her coat pocket and was fumbling for the pencil. She quickly scribbled down a few words:

selkies will take me 2 HL, have 2 go NOW,
SORRY! Lv, K

She stuffed the pad and pencil into her coat pocket, and together with her boots and glasses, shoved them into the crevice where she had been hiding.

By the time she ran to the water's edge, the last selkie was nearly into her sealskin. Like magic it appeared to zip together at the seam as she rolled to the ground and hustled with awkward seal undulations to join the others in the water.

Once again Kira dove in, muttering, "I'm so sorry, Mrs. Doyle. Sorry, Mom. Sorry, Dad. Sorry, Cody. What the heck am I doing? Am I crazy?"

Ahead of her the five slick black bodies swam along the surface, moonlight bouncing off their shiny backs. Kira pumped her tail hard to keep them in sight. As she caught up they spun around her, barking and clapping their flippers together as if congratulating her. And like her selkie companions with their seal memories, Kira's brain switched into merrow drive. The joy of swimming vanquished any guilt or anxiety she'd felt on land. She had an important mission and that was all that mattered.

Chapter Five–
Through the Whirlwater

The first part of the journey was quiet, uneventful. Between the strong moonlight and her excellent underwater vision, Kira had no trouble seeing her surroundings. The seaweeds and grasses were bluer than in daylight, but their gentle swaying in the current made her feel welcome and at home. As on her previous excursions, it felt like she'd always lived underwater.

The seals swam quickly and efficiently, not like the ones she'd seen playing with the bottle. They took a course that Kira tried to memorize, but she soon realized the path would be impossible to remember. There were no unusual features to note. They turned right, heading south at first, then swung into the open ocean. The ground sloped down steeply until everything melted into solid darkness. No more seaweed, only a few fish that passed close by.

Unlike seals, Kira did not need to breathe air when she was underwater in her merrow form. She noticed they rose up to the surface to take in air more often than the dolphins. Kira didn't mind. She usually followed them up and had a look around. In the darkness, out in the open ocean, there was not much to see. Occasionally she noticed pinpoints of light on the water, but without her glasses they were fuzzy spots. If there was no land nearby, she assumed the lights belonged to ships. As the hours passed, the sky lost its inky blackness. Sometime during that predawn greyness, she noticed the ground rising up, and she heard the rumble of distant surf. They were nearing dry land again.

One of the seals startled Kira by turning around and coming face to face with her. The seal barked sharply then turned away. The others pressed around her and forced a change in direction, heading directly toward shore. They began to bark in sharp, staccato bursts, an urgency in their tone. Kira beat her tail hard to keep up with the leader, and the rest like a peloton of racing cyclists encircled her. She hadn't seen the danger yet, but she sensed it nearby. Two of the seals put their heads under each of her arms and she felt herself flying through the water as if she had grown wings with rocket thrusters. All six of them rode in on a final enormous wave and tumbled onto a narrow, stony beach.

"Ouch!" she cried, rolling with the momentum and smacking into a wall of rock. The others spread out along the base of the cliff and faced the water. Kira stared out over the grey seascape, straining to see what had been chasing them. She tried to remember what kind of large, aggressive sea creatures were normally found along that part of the Atlantic coastline. Besides the giant squid, which rarely came into such shallow waters, there wasn't much out there. Great white sharks perhaps, but they were not common either.

Then she saw the faintest movement cutting through the surface, parallel to the shoreline. First travelling left, then right, disappearing, then there it was again. A pale triangular tip. The rough waves barely disturbed its course, back and forth. A determined predator, one to be feared by fish, seals, humans, and merrows. It had to be a great white. Kira shivered, soaked and cold in her human form, huddled with her back to the cliff. Was the tide moving in or out? Was the shark waiting for the water to trap his prey?

Kira looked behind her and up the side of the cliff. She might be able to climb up far enough to stay out of harm's way. But not the seals. She groaned. She understood now how much danger they were being exposed to on this journey. Just to help her, a stranger. But they had known the risks from the start, she thought. Perhaps this was normal for them, she tried to console herself. She hated the thought of all the people and animals who might suffer because she was so pig-headed about this quest. Why couldn't she just let things be?

But she knew why. She firmly believed that her

family and many others were being badly mistreated on a horrid prison island. Kira had always had a strong sense of justice and fairness. She had never given in to bullies herself, and would not stand by if she saw them picking on others. She and Cody were similar that way. He was a geek and seemed proud of it, and somehow the bullies left him alone. His good size probably helped, but maybe the confidence he had was more of a deterrent. He didn't care what other kids said or thought about him.

Kira tried to judge if the beach was disappearing, or if the tide was going out. She had the sense that it was creeping in, but very slowly. She studied the faces of the seals. They had settled, were scratching and grooming themselves as if this was a scheduled rest stop. Kira perked up. Maybe it *was* a usual resting place. They had been swimming all night since they left the small cove, perhaps five hours. Then again, clock time was fuzzy underwater. The moon was nearly gone, and sunrise not far off, based on the softening colour of the night sky.

As a pink dawn broke over the dark ocean it was obvious that the tide was slipping out. There was no sign of Mr. Shark and the seals were restless. Kira stood up slowly and stared out at the water. With her poor eyesight on land she was at a disadvantage when scanning the surface for trouble. One of the seals, the youngest, most slender member of the herd, moved down to the water's edge and slipped in. The others kept their heads raised as they watched from shore. Within a few seconds the black head poked out of the water and barked once.

The four seals yawned and made whining, growling sounds as they re-entered the water. The last one turned her grey muzzle to face Kira, opened her mouth, and made a soft *ahh* sound before she dove in. Kira took that to be the all-clear signal and followed. As she caught up to the pack, she noted for the first time that the last seal was a softer black, a sort of charcoal grey all over with white whiskers. She assumed this was the oldest of the group, Coralene's sister, Solina. She crossed her fingers as she swam, hoping no harm would come to this ancient seal. Babbling Bill's sister-in-law, as it were. The thought made her smile.

They caught their breakfast as they came upon schools of small fish that lived in those waters. They were heading back into the deeper ocean again, and Kira noticed that the sea life was different from that in the shallower waters near the coast. She particularly liked the pale blue fish that swam in smaller groups. They were trickier to catch, but very tasty. How would she describe them to Cody? Somewhat nutty, with a hint of pepper? Yes, he'd like that, being a foodie. He'd also be able to tell her the exact species name, their usual habitat, what they ate, and everything about their biology that had been reported by marine specialists. Kira thought it might be nice to bring back some new facts for him, things that had not been observed or recorded yet. With no way to write things down, she'd have to memorize all these details. For instance, the way they scattered when they were trying to evade predators—like herself.

Yes, she thought sadly, she and the great white shark had that in common. Every living thing had to eat. She wondered if there were any vegetarian or vegan merrows. The ones she knew loved their seafood, but, like humans, there might be a few odd merrows who wouldn't eat sea meat. Kira liked seaweed, but it would be a boring diet if that was all you ate, she thought. Then again, she hadn't tried all the different sea greens out there. Somehow she thought her parents might not approve of a vegetarian mermaid, especially her fisherman father.

The group of six swam through that day and another night. They stopped to rest one more time on shore, a sandy cove with a small salt marsh nearly surrounded by stubby twisted pines. Kira found tiny fingerling fish in the marsh and tried to eat one. She decided after spitting it out that fresh, raw fish tasted much better underwater. The seals barked at her, rolled on their backs, clapped their flippers, and swatted the ground with their tails. Kira giggled at their antics while they were sealaughing at her.

By the time they returned to the water it was serious business again, and, if anything, the pace picked up. Kira felt charged with energy though she hadn't slept at all and had eaten very little in a day and a half. The current was stronger now and the water colder. The one time she decided to take a peek above water, there was no land in sight, no lights to be seen.

Kira was grateful to the seals for showing her the way, but she missed the dolphins who were able to communicate with her. She wanted to know so many things about them and about this place they were approaching. How far were they from Hildaland, for instance? When would they know they were near?

The seals slowed as she had these thoughts and she wondered if they could read minds even though they couldn't speak in their seal forms. They moved closer together and she swam as near to them as she could. Their flapping tails occasionally brushed her nose. Ahead she could make out a lighter patch in the dark water. The seals did not seem alarmed, only wary. Was it a huge grey whale? Kira shivered with excitement. That would be something to see, to make Cody's eyes pop out of his head. Whatever it was, it was a monster in size, reaching as high up and low down as Kira could see. Like a solid wall. Maybe they were at the border of Hildaland's waters.

The seals came to a sudden stop. The wall was actually approaching them, growing in size and brightness. There were no features to make out, no outline of a shape, nothing recognizable. Was it a ship, a submarine? The only sound Kira could hear was her own heart, thrashing in her chest.

The seals appeared confused. One began to rise, another to go deeper. The other three twirled in place. Then Kira could hear another sound over her throbbing heart, a high, wavering note. No, many notes, all high register, growing louder as the wall continued to brighten.

Kira had no idea what they were, only that there were thousands of them as the wall resolved into bright dots. In the same instant she noticed that the brightness continued to the right as far as she could see, but on the left there was a fuzzy edge where it faded to darkness.

A decision had to be made, and fast. "Follow me!" Kira shouted at the seals. "Follow me! Now!"

The seals stopped moving and turned to face her. They heard, but did they understand, and would they follow? Kira waved her hand, pointing to the left as she swam in that direction, away from the growing, screaming wall. She didn't look back, and she swam as fast as she could. The ear-piercing sound was painful to her and she wondered how the seals could tolerate the noise.

Kira pinned her arms to her sides and beat her tail with all the strength she could summon. She wanted to look at the wall but was afraid. Her curiosity won and she glanced to her right without breaking speed. She gasped. Snakes? Eels? Yellow, striped with luminescent green, millions of them, swimming as if they were one gigantic, monstrous organism.

Kira focussed on the darkness opening up ahead. The wall now had a well-defined edge, but the eels were also more distinct, their mouths gaping open. She was certain she could see dagger-like teeth lining the mouths. So many mouths.

Kira knew she was slowing down, and she wasn't sure if she had the energy to clear that mass of shrieking eels. Even if they weren't hungry, she was certain that running into so many of them at one time could be fatal. She pumped harder at the thought of all those sharp knives shredding her body and suddenly she was on the other side, in darkness. She whirled around at a safe distance and watched them stream by.

Where were the seals? She looked around, heard a bark above her head, and there they were, all five of them. Kira clapped her hands and the seals snapped their flippers. As the last of the glowing yellow eels disappeared they reunited and headed up to the surface.

Kira laughed with relief while the seals gulped air and shook their heads. She should teach the ladies a high five, she thought. But when she scanned around she gasped at a familiar sight behind her. A cloud bank hovered in the distance. Perhaps it was only a bit of fog out here in the middle of the Atlantic Ocean. Then the seals turned to face her and began to bark, all together. They turned as one, facing the cloud bank, and continued to bark. As if on a signal, they became quiet and turned to her again.

"This is it, isn't it?" She didn't dare speak the name. Kira knew this was the end of her escort. She suddenly felt insecure, alone, and not sure she wanted to proceed. But again as if sensing her thoughts, the seals began to swim on the surface toward the cloud, and Kira followed. They hadn't finished with her yet. As they drew nearer, Kira noticed sparkles within the cloud. She had the strange sensation that her hair above the water was lifting off her scalp. It reminded her of static electricity, like pulling off a wool sweater then touching her metal locker at school. Snap! Then she realized that the sparkles were sparks, that the cloud was charged with electricity. If only she had Cody's brain for science so she could figure out how that could be, and if it was dangerous.

Then Solina gave small bark and they all dipped below the surface. Kira followed suit, and found herself facing an underwater wonder. Ahead of them was another wall, this one made of water swirling vertically, up and around and down in great circles and figure eights. She could feel the turbulence where they hovered, buffeting them, neither drawing them in nor repelling them. The whirlwater, Solina had called it. They had reached the underwater border of Hildaland.

The seals barked softly and swam around Kira a few times, brushing her gently with their flippers and whiskers. Kira touched each one and said, "Thank you," over and over until they finally turned and swam off together, leaving her alone. She watched them until they disappeared, fighting the urge to go after them. Was she really brave enough to carry on by herself? Finally she turned to face her next challenge, an unnatural wonder.

Kira did not know how long she hovered in front of the whirlwater. It looked like it could mince her up then spit out the pieces on the other side, like the spinning turbines in a dam powered by falling water. She swam a little closer, ready to retreat if it started to suck her in. A few feet from the whirlwater she felt its force—it stopped her cold. No matter how hard she beat her tail, an invisible wall blocked her from moving forward. Kira backed up, paused, then rushed toward it. She bounced back as if she'd jumped on a trampoline. Strangely, though, there was no sensation of contact.

Kira scanned to the left and right to see if there was a visible break, but the wall of water went on and on until it faded in the murky green distance. Most likely it curved around the island. She decided to swim around the whirlwater to look for a natural entrance. There had to be a way in, because she'd been through twice before, once entering with a finfolk escort, and once on her own when she escaped them. She tried to recall any signs of the whirlwater at the time, and could not. Perhaps this water wall did not go all the way around. Or perhaps a passage opened when finfolk went in, and it didn't prevent anyone from swimming out.

Still questioning her sanity, but not her purpose, Kira began her circumnavigation of the Hildaland whirlwater. From time to time she approached the great wall to test it for openings she could not see. Each time she was stopped. Once in a while she swam to the surface but the view was always the same—she was on the outside of a cloud bank that sizzled with charged particles. She had no way of knowing how far she had gone since there were no landmarks above, or seamarks below, to gauge the distance. For all she knew she had already been around it and was now swimming in circles.

By the time Kira surfaced and realized that night was approaching again, she growled in frustration. Exasperated, she heaved her tail out of the water and smacked it on the surface. The resulting spray of water cleared off a semicircle of mist to reveal a sheet of calm water, not the turbulence she had expected from the whirlwater below.

Kira approached the cloud with caution, trying to stay on top of the water to avoid the currents beneath. She barely fluttered her tail as she floated into and was swallowed by the electrified mist. Her scalp prickled from the static—nothing like the jolts she'd felt on land, though. Kira had been holding her breath, and began to let it out in short bursts. She tried to breathe in, but the solid blanket of cloud seemed to have squeezed the air out of the atmosphere, suffocating and blinding her. Panic rose in her throat, choking the scream she could hear in her brain: *Get me out of here, I can't breathe!* A deep, bone-seeking cold paralyzed her body—she could not move a muscle.

Kira floated on the water, her eyes closed, her face turned up to the sky. She felt warmth on her cheeks and brightness filtering through her eyelids. Slowly, she opened her eyes and the mauve colour that filled her sight was unexpected and beautiful. For a moment she simply stared up, her brain still frozen, her body sluggish. She felt her fingers twitch, then her chest heaved and she took in a deep breath. Thoughts began to flood her thawing brain. She was not sure she could move, not sure if she had gone through or been spit back out. Was she even in one piece? Was she alive?

Kira lifted her head and swung her tail down to look over the water. The cloud bank was behind her at some distance. Ahead was a familiar rocky island. She had made it through! How long had it taken, she wondered. She remembered the panic, but for now she was as calm as the smooth sea around her. She replayed what had just happened, tried to remember what she had planned to do next. Kira realized she had no plan—she only wanted to find her parents. She remembered the selkies' advice. It was time to go under, to watch for the sentinels of Hildaland. She knew she should be hyper-aware, suspicious, and perhaps frightened, but all she felt was relief that she had survived this far. She was ready to face anything that Hildaland would throw her way.

Chapter Six–King Currin and Queen Calista

The terrain below appeared no different than the deep Atlantic waters she had just passed through. The sea floor was laced with valleys carpeted in waving seaweed and bordered by rock outcrops that formed rolling hills. Small fish of various colours swam in clusters; the larger fish swam alone. Kira headed for a valley and stayed close to the top of the plants, prepared to dive down into the mass of weeds if she needed to hide. She moved toward the island, constantly surveying the waters on all sides and above her. There were no large objects to be seen, no sharks, orcas, squid, or finfolk, as far as she could tell.

Soon the rumble of crashing surf let her know she was close to the shore. At the same time she noticed two dark shadows to the right and ahead of her. Kira slipped down into a clump of broad-leafed plants, hoping she hadn't been spotted. The shadows took distinct forms as they neared, long and sleek and silvery. Sharks, with single black stripes on their sides. Kira had never seen that type before—one more species to report to Cody. They were somewhat smaller than the great white beast that had chased her and the selkies onto land. This pair swam past her hiding spot and she watched them vanish into dark grey water on her far left.

Almost immediately another creature emerged just below where the sharks had disappeared. This one was much larger and swimming faster. An orca! Kira had never seen one before. She gasped, awed by the flashy white on black of the massive whale. Peeking from between the broad, sheltering leaves, she tracked the movement of the predatory mammal as it swam directly above her, for a moment blocking all the light. Kira had no idea how well or how far an orca could see. She remained frozen in place, only her eyes moving as she watched the huge monster fade away to her right.

Kira waited a long while to see if there were any other sharks or orcas patrolling the area. The selkies had warned her about the Hildaland security system. She was preparing to leave her lair when she noticed a long narrow object far up above her. She watched it for a while, noting that it was rigid and seemed to be floating on the surface, pushed by the waves toward the shore. It was definitely not swimming. Probably an old log, she thought, a common sight along many east coast shorelines.

She pushed off from her seaweed bed and resumed her swim, feeling more confident that she could reach the island unnoticed. She swam quickly, could feel the tug of the tide helping her along. The sea floor was rising rapidly up to the beach. Kira felt both excitement and fear, and beat her tail harder.

The log that had been floating behind her suddenly appeared ahead and above her. In the next moment it became a torpedo with a dark, sinister face and a gaping mouth full of sharp, silvery teeth, shooting straight toward her. Finfolk! Shape shifters, she remembered, too late. Strong arms gripped her; she was caught. Not by just one finfolk; she was surrounded by three or four. Where had they come from?

Unlike the younger finfolk Kira had seen, the adults had fins all over their bodies, black, grey, green, with streamers of seaweed hanging from them. A spiked fin poked out of their heads, like the triangular back fin of a shark. Up close they were the ugliest creatures Kira had ever seen, exuding a stench that made her want to retch.

Kira and her captors were thrown onto the beach by the breaking waves. Her tail evaporated and she found herself on her hands and knees in the sand. To her horror, the finfolk also morphed as they crawled up onto the beach. Two short, chunky legs with curved claws emerged from the trunks of their bodies, while their arms shortened and became front legs. They had let go of her. Could they run? Could they climb the trees less than fifty feet from the water's edge? Kira pushed herself up and leaped over them, sprinting as fast as she could, her eyes fixed on the tree just ahead of her. She was at the tree, then up the trunk, grabbing at branches, pulling herself up. She clung to a sturdy branch high in the tree, hidden amongst the leaves. Finally, breathless and shaking, she dared to look down.

The finfolk had reached the base of the tree. They surrounded it, lashing their barbed tails and looking up with their long, narrow faces. Like mutant crocodiles they grumbled and snapped their pointed teeth.

Kira was puzzled by what happened next. Or what didn't happen. The lizardlike finfolk clawed at the tree trunk, but none of them tried to climb it. Perhaps they couldn't. She heard them grunting as they milled about, but they spoke no recognizable words. After a few moments they all left, growling as they waddled off on their stumpy legs.

Kira remained in the tree long after she had stopped shaking, wondering when or if the finfolk would return to search for her. All she could hear were the sounds of the surf and the occasional chirping bird or screeching gull. She'd have to come down sooner or later. Her arms were cramping and she was exhausted. Slowly she crept into the lower branches where she could have a better look around. She saw the sandy beach leading up to steep dunes sprinkled with tall grasses waving in the breeze. There were no buildings, no boats or wharf, no people, no finfolk.

Kira gazed out over the waters and tried to focus on the surface. She saw the distinct triangular fins of sharks cruising along the shore. Maybe not sharks, she thought, but those pointy-headed finfolk disguised as logs. She remembered Cody reading from the book, how they could make themselves appear as floating chunks of wood or clumps of weeds. The female finfolk were even better at deception, sometimes pretending to be mermaids. Like the young finfolk friends of her cousins.

And like Queen Shree, her black hair, the small, shifting eyes, the clawlike fingers. Kira was more certain than ever that Queen Shree had been behind the ambush and capture of her parents all those years ago.

She shut her eyes for a moment. She was worn out from several days of continuous swimming and hardly any sleep or food. For some reason she had more energy underwater than she did on land. Kira settled into the crook of her tree where she would not tumble out if she fell asleep. She took a deep breath, closed her eyes, and gave in to her exhaustion.

"Kira!"

The shout nearly startled her out of the tree. She gripped her branch tightly and tried to locate the source of the voice. A woman's voice, someone who knew her name! Or did she just dream it?

"Kira, are you here? We won't harm you, dear. You can show yourself," the woman spoke in soothing tones.

This was not a dream, and Kira was not buying any promises. It had to be a trick to get her down, probably a finfolk in human disguise, she thought. No, she would not be fooled again. She would remain quiet and stay put.

"Ah, there you are. It really is you." The woman stood directly under Kira's branch, her hands raised in the air as if welcoming the sun. Kira sucked in her breath, hardly daring to look. The woman suddenly bent her head and her shoulders began to shake.

A tall man appeared and put his arms around the sobbing woman. He looked up and met Kira's eyes with his startling green ones. She immediately thought of Nim, whose eyes were similar but more grey.

"Kira, it *is* you," he said, his tone deep and quiet. He was not smiling as he stroked the woman's bent head.

Kira was stunned. She couldn't have spoken if she'd wished to. Below her were two people with long, wavy hair, the woman's golden, the man's a fawn brown. If this man was related to Nim, this could be her father. Kira shivered, felt her eyes burning.

The woman raised her head and Kira looked into her large azure eyes. Kira gasped. She knew that face! She felt her hands tremble, felt her grip loosen on the branch. Before her the leaves became swimming green fish, and then darkness closed in on her.

She awakened on the beach, smelling an unfamiliar fragrance—some exotic flower, perhaps. Her eyes opened to see a delicate chin and mouth, small nose, and large blue eyes, all upside down.

"She has awakened, Currin, look," the woman said, touching Kira's tangled wet hair. The woman's own long blonde curls lay over Kira's shoulders like a shawl.

"Wh-what happened?" Kira stuttered and tried to sit. The golden lady supported her as she pushed herself up.

"I think you fainted from the shock, darling. I am so sorry we frightened you," she apologized.

Kira stared at her and the man standing behind her. She was waiting for them to transform into disgusting reptilian creatures. But they didn't waver.

"We managed to catch you," the man said, chuckling. "You are more solid than you appear."

Kira cleared her throat. "Are you my, um, my—"

"Parents? Yes, Kira, we are your parents," the solemn man said. "And we are glad to finally know you are alive and well. But also sad that you are here."

Kira stared at him, confused.

"We are prisoners on this island, and will likely remain here for the rest of our lives," he said. "I am sorry that you will now be a prisoner with us."

"Oh, but she is with us! That is the most important thing!" the woman protested.

"It's not your fault," Kira said. "I came looking for you. And I found you!"

The man shook his head. "It is *our* fault that we were captured and brought here."

"Oh, Currin, how were we to know that Shree was behind it? That Nim, your own brother, may have betrayed us?" the woman said.

"Half-brother," he corrected her. "Because I should have listened to you when you suspected Shree's true identity. This is all my fault. And now poor Kira is also trapped." He turned away for a moment, shaking his head.

"Do not mind him, Kira. We have been arguing about this for years. I am sure this is awkward for you. You have land parents, do you not?"

Kira nodded.

"Have they been good to you?" Her voice quivered.

"Yes, they have. They didn't want me to go to the sea, but they never explained why. They wanted me to be safe, I guess…" Kira dropped her head, realizing that by now they would know she was gone, probably for good. She felt awful.

"Kira, my darling. That is what all good parents wish for their children. That is why we left you in their care when we were captured. While you are here, we promise to care for you and keep you safe."

Kira could no longer hold back her tears. In a short space of time, she had found her real parents, but lost the two who had raised and loved her. And now she had lost her freedom as well. Calista put her arms around her long-lost daughter and let her weep.

Chapter Seven-
Hildaland

In spite of all the excitement, Kira slept well that first night in the home of her newfound parents. The next morning they took her on a tour. In her exhausted state upon arrival she hadn't paid much attention to their village. The houses were small and came in a variety of shapes. Calista explained that the type of house depended on whether the builders were human or merrow. Kira guessed correctly that merrows built the round ones, and humans built the houses with straight sides and flat or peaked roofs.

The colours were the drab, natural tones of wood, rock, and various materials found on the island. Some of the rock houses had frames and beams of wood. One house was made from rocks and shells plastered together with a seaweed cement. Over time, Currin told her, the humans and merrows had learned from each other. They began to build better, stronger homes that would withstand the worst weather. Calista and Currin lived in one of the more modern houses using a blend of styles.

Kira also learned that there were two villages on the island, about four hundred inhabitants in all, and that it was an ancient place. "You mean," she asked, "that

Hildaland has been a finfolk prison for centuries?"

"We do not know how long," Currin said, "but it has been a prison as long as our merrow folk can remember. The heavy white fog that always surrounds the island has kept all human-made boats out, unless the finfolk bring them in."

Calista added, "*Hildaland* means hidden island. It is lost in the mists. The only way to find the island is from underwater."

Kira thought back to her terrifying passage through the mists, floating on the electrified surface. She would not recommend that trip to anyone. And apparently the island could not be seen from the air, since it did not show up on any maps.

"Have you ever tried to escape?" she asked.

"At first that was all we thought about," said Currin. "Every day, all day long, we planned our escape. But we simply could not find a way out. And those who tried, well, they failed."

"Some returned soon enough," said Calista when she saw Kira's concern. "They couldn't get very far. The waters are infested with sharks and killer whales, and, of course, finfolk. They also command an army of giant squid who live farther out in deeper waters." Calista shuddered.

"But they can't be everywhere at once," Kira suggested. "We could outswim them if we timed it just right, we could—"

"No dear, that's not possible. Not anymore," Calista said, shaking her head. "Even if we could sneak past all of them, Currin and I can no longer change back." She covered her face with her hands.

Kira nodded. "Of course, I knew that. Oh, I didn't tell you. My mother Bess, my adoptive mother, is a mermaid. I just found out this summer. She can't change either."

Calista clapped her hands together and laughed. "A mermaid, how wonderful! And your father?"

"He's a human, a fisherman. He found me."

Currin gave a sad smile. "And of course they tried to keep you from the water. To no avail. And we must do the same and insist you not enter the water. It is far too dangerous, even if you can transform."

"Is it safe to walk everywhere on land? Where are all the finfolk?"

They had been sitting at a table in the kitchen and Currin stood up and began to pace. "They like to stay on the other side of the island, near Digger's Hill. That's what we call the mine at the base of the old volcano, where we dig out the silver ore. It used to be called Silver City, but no one calls it that now. Only the miners with no families live there. The finfolk live underwater and only come out to supervise the mining and smelting of ore into silver."

Currin explained that this was how the prisoners were expected to earn their keep. So, thought Kira, this part of Cody's finfolk description was accurate. They loved their silver. She wondered what their homes looked like, and if their underwater palace was made of silver. Perhaps some of them capped their teeth with silver, like the finfolkling who had smiled at her with metal gleaming between his lips.

Currin told her that on land the finfolk were handicapped with their short, thick limbs and awkward claws. They needed slaves to mine the ore and process it into pure silver metal, labourers with longer legs and arms who could dig with shovels and carry loads. Humans and landed merrows were perfect for those jobs. Kira was thankful that she wouldn't have to see the hideous finfolk often, if at all.

"I must warn you, Kira," Currin added, "that they may look clumsy and slow on land, but they can run faster than you think. And they have been known to badly injure prisoners. Some people do not recover from their poisonous wounds. So avoid them if you can."

Kira shuddered, remembering their snapping jaws and claws raking at the tree she had climbed.

Learning that there was no easy or obvious way off the island was depressing news for Kira, though she had no way of knowing this before she had started off. It was hard to believe she was a prisoner as she walked about the village, meeting her parents' friends and their children. There were elderly people, there were toddlers, there were babies. Long ago, the village was named Stayawhile, which changed to Nowhereville as more new slaves arrived. Eventually it was referred to as Noville, a place that many wished had never existed. The village looked and felt like any other community on mainland. Except for the perpetual offshore fog ring, the oddly shaped houses, and the lack of any motor vehicles.

Hildaland also had no electricity, but there was wood, coal, and oil to heat homes and cook meals. Most families kept small backyard gardens; some kept chickens. There was a bakery, a small restaurant, a sawmill, a weavery and tailor shop, and a school for children in Noville.

Digger's Hill had wood and metal shops, and a pottery studio. And a large boarding house for unmarried miners and other workers. Currin avoided the word "slaves," Kira noticed.

"We eat well enough," he said. "The finfolk provide fish because they won't allow us to use boats. Besides the chickens for eggs and meat, we have wild rabbits for meat and pelts, and we keep goats for milk and sheep for wool." There were also a few ponies to pull carts, but there were no dogs or cats.

"Do you use money here?" Kira asked.

Currin laughed. "No, we trade and barter. Much like we did back at home, in Merhaven, under the sea. We do not have our own silver, though in the past a few humans tried to hide silver from the finfolk. I suppose they expected to escape one day and return home rich. But no one escapes from Hildaland. Money and silver are worthless here."

"So why do finfolk want so much silver? What do they do with it?"

"Some like to cap their teeth with silver. They may use it for spear tips or decoration. Maybe they use it for trade. We do not know where they take it once it leaves the island."

Kira wished she could share all these facts with Cody. He would be thrilled to learn the truth about Hildaland, and how people lived and created their own world in the middle of the Atlantic.

"Do you have a map of Hildaland?"

Currin chuckled. "A map? I have seen a map at the mine but we keep no maps here in Noville. You have a curious mind. An explorer like I was in my youth," he said. "I think I can draw a map for you, if you like."

They looked for paper, which Kira discovered was not easy to come by since everything was made by hand or came in on stolen boats. Finally they stepped outside and found a level spot of ground covered by sand. Currin began to draw with a sturdy stick. The island was roughly oval-shaped, with the volcano at the north end. The smelter was on the edge of the north shore, and Digger's Hill to the southeast of the smelter. Near the centre of the island, on the south slope of the dormant volcano, were the cleared sheep pastures and dairy barns. Noville was nestled in the southeast corner of the island. Currin added the cloud ring at the very end.

"So is this to scale? I mean the distance to the cloud bank, and the size of the island?" Kira asked.

"Yes, I believe so," Currin said. "I walk this path to and from the mine most every day."

"How far is that?"

"Hmm. About one hundred and sixty lengths of Merhaven."

Kira stared at him. Of course, they didn't measure in metres or yards underwater. She tried to remember how long Merhaven was. She recalled it was approximately square, maybe fifty metres long. She did the math. That would make the island about eight kilometres long and five kilometres wide. The cloud bank would be three kilometres offshore according to the map. It was probably useless information, but she already had plans to explore the island, especially the shoreline and the centre.

Toward the end of her first full day on Hildaland, Kira asked her parents how they knew she had arrived on the island, and where to find her.

"Any unusual activity on the beaches is always noticed by someone, and news travels quickly. We were rather expecting your arrival," Currin said.

Kira's eyes went wide with surprise. "You were?"

"Yes, a few months ago two young merrows were captured," Currin continued. "We heard the boy was quite indignant, and insisted he was a prince. When an island elder asked him to name his parents, we knew at once who he and his sister were."

Aha, Kira thought; her cousins had been taken prisoner after all.

Calista put her arm around Kira's shoulders. "Borin was born just a few months before you were, Kira. We were already here when Amelie was born at Merhaven so we didn't know she existed. They spoke of their cousin who had escaped capture, and when they mentioned your name, I nearly fainted."

"You mean *you* gave me the name Kira?" She thought her adoptive parents had named her.

"Why yes, we named you Kira. You were just over a year old when we lost you."

"Did I already know my name then?"

"Of course you did. Perhaps you spoke your name so your new parents knew what to call you. Merrowlings start talking earlier than human babies," Calista said.

"Or," Currin said, "the fishermen might have heard

me yell your name after I slipped you into their net. I had spotted their fishing boat just before the finfolk ambushed us. When I knew we were overpowered, that we could not escape, I swam to their boat. I knew our fate would be grim. I only wanted you to be safe and not in the hands of our enemies."

Kira felt bad. Her merrow father had tried to save her by handing her over to humans for safekeeping. Her land parents had tried to keep her from returning to the dangers of the sea, but they did not succeed either. Perhaps her arrival on Hildaland was meant to be.

By the end of her first day on Hildaland, Kira felt overwhelmed with all that she had seen and learned from her royal parents. She had told them a little about her life on the mainland, and her visit to Merhaven. She could see how agitated Calista became when she mentioned Shree's name, so Kira didn't want to say anything more about her cousins in case it upset her further. But she also didn't want to run into them by accident. In fact, right then Kira thought she never wanted to see them again, but she did ask where they were.

"I hear they are living in Digger's Hill, and that the finfolk did not want them staying here in Noville," Currin said. "Men from both villages work in the mine, and that's where we share news when there is any." Apparently news travelled fast on Hildand; no need for telephones or newspapers on such a small place.

Kira was relieved that her cousins did not live nearby. She still wondered if they had expected her and not them to be captured when they got to Hildaland that summer. Treacherous like their parents, Kira thought.

Before she went to bed that night, Kira felt she had to settle something that had been bothering her since her arrival the day before. "I have one more question for you," she said, looking down at her hands. "Um, what should I call you?"

Calista, who was sitting in a chair, knitting socks, smiled at Currin. "What do you call your land parents, Kira?"

Kira met Calista's large blue eyes, twinkling at her. "Mom and Dad." She suddenly pictured her mother desperately searching for her, and her father, dejected and afraid, blaming himself for her disappearance. It was all she could do not to burst into tears. At the same time she was annoyed with herself for being so emotional, and hoped she wouldn't feel like crying every day from then on.

"You are growing up so fast, Kira, you are a young lady now. Please call us Calista and Currin." Currin nodded in agreement and patted her head like her dad Cillian did.

"Okay. Goodnight, uh, Calista and Currin. And thank you for everything." Before turning away Kira noticed

Calista tearing up, so she hurried to her room. She didn't want them to see her own tears.

A few days after Kira's arrival, news came that a small tsunami had hit the mainland shore. The deep sea earthquake that created the wave had also destroyed Finfolkaheen, the centre of the finfolk world. What was most worrisome was a rumour that the finfolk planned to take over the merrows' palace of crystal as their new home.

All the merrows were upset to hear the news, but Calista and Currin were the most distraught. Merhaven, their ancestral home, was the heart of the merrow kingdom on this side of the Atlantic. To imagine those awful, greedy finfolk taking it over was unbearable. Kira heard Calista weeping at night, wondering aloud to Currin what was to become of their ancestral kingdom, and of all the merrows.

Kira knew that not all merrows lived in the palace. Probably most of those loyal to her parents left when they had disappeared many years ago. She wondered what would happen to Nim and Shree when the finfolk moved in. She supposed they would stay, since Shree was one of them anyway. Maybe that was the plan all along. She also wondered why, if Shree was a finfolk, they had not come looking for their children. Unless this was part of a bigger plan and Borin and Amelie were expected to remain on Hildaland for some time, perhaps as spies. Yes, that would fit the finfolk pattern of treachery.

Kira tried not to feel depressed, hearing Calista's grief in the next room, knowing how naïve she'd been to think that she, a thirteen-year-old mermaid, could go off on her own to rescue her royal parents from a prison island where they had been trapped for twelve years. And no doubt she had broken the hearts of her parents and disappointed two dear friends. She had really messed up this time. Kira began to despair that she'd never see her home again.

Chapter Eight–
A New Home

Kira was not allowed to mope for long. Calista made sure she got to know a number of other children in the village by introducing Kira to all the neighbours and enrolling her in school. Classes were held five mornings out of every week; afternoons were reserved for skills training. On Hildaland, a week was six days, not seven. The first day she walked into her school classroom Kira almost burst out laughing. All the merrows, with their large, round, weak eyes, sat in the front rows, closer to the teacher and the writing board. Guessing who was a merrow and who was a human was a game she and Cody used to play back at home.

Meanwhile, her parents both worked like every other able-bodied adult in the village. Calista made cloth and mended clothing, skills she learned when she first arrived. As a merrow queen she had not been required to do any labour, but now she had no choice. Over time, she told Kira, she had come to enjoy her work. It distracted her and kept her from thinking too much about Merhaven, about the home and life and child she had lost.

The job was challenging, since everything had to be

made from the material around them. Wool clipped from the sheep was spun into yarn, sometimes dyed with natural pigments found in wild and garden plants, then woven into cloth for warm winter garments. For summer wear, special sea grasses were softened, then split into threads and woven into linen sheets. Women from the village made the cloth, cut it, and sewed it into clothing by hand.

Calista had started as a mender, but she was so skilled as a cloth-maker she now directed the weaving studio. Thanks to her eye for colour, the clothing she designed and made was in demand by all the islanders. Her home was filled with the beautiful wooden bowls, stone tools, and utensils made by skilled woodworkers and stone-cutters, traded for her blankets, shawls, and clothing.

Currin worked in the silver mine like most of the other men. Everyone knew he was the rightful merrow king, but he wished to be treated like all the others. Every evening he returned to their small house, filthy from digging and so exhausted he barely had an appetite. Kira asked why he had to work so long and hard.

"We have little choice, Kira. If we don't deliver the silver quota they set for us, we don't get fish to eat. There aren't enough livestock or wild animals on Hildaland to keep us all properly fed. We would starve without their fish."

On Hildaland, Kira's parents were common folk, not the royalty they had once been in their underwater kingdom. The daily pattern of parents going off to their hard and tedious labour and Kira going off to school was really no different from her life on the mainland, except, of course, that it was completely without electricity and modern conveniences. Life on Hildaland had slid back in time and was far more primitive than even the model pioneer village she had visited on a school trip two years ago. For one thing, it was missing something even pioneer schools had—books. They also had no paper in their school; there was no reading and very little writing. Mrs. McIver taught them many things about the mainland, and a few things about the sea, but it all had to be memorized. School for Kira became repetitive and boring and she couldn't wait to be outside again at the end of classes.

After one particularly dreary day, Kira found herself longing for her mainland home, for her parents, for Cody, and even for Mrs. Doyle. She still felt bad about disappearing on them and tried not to think about how upset they must feel, not knowing what had happened to her. Poor Mrs. Doyle: first her husband lost, now Kira. Then she realized she had not asked about Captain Doyle, if he and his crew had ended up on Hildaland or if they'd truly been lost at sea. That night she asked Currin if he had heard the name.

"Captain Harvey Doyle?" Currin said, running his hand through his long, curly hair. "There is a miner in Digger's Hill who goes by Doyle. And another one they call Captain. Both work the other shifts so I do not know them well."

"Could you ask if they might know Yvette Doyle? She's the librarian who helped me find the selkies."

Two days later Kira came home from school to find a strange man sitting on a wooden stool outside their house. He wore a weathered wool cap and had a bushy brown beard streaked with grey. She approached with caution, taught from an early age to be wary of strangers. He rose slowly, as if he was very old. When Kira looked into his pale eyes she noticed the deep shadows below and realized that the man was simply weary.

"Are you Miss Kira?"

She nodded. "Yes."

"Your father, Currin, told me you know Yvette Doyle, a librarian."

Kira nodded again and held her breath, unable to speak.

The man offered his calloused hand to her. "Captain Harvey Doyle at your service, Miss Kira."

They talked well into the evening, eventually joined by Currin and Calista, who insisted that Captain Doyle have supper with them. He described how giant squid had attacked his boat and how they had been dragged through the fog bank to Hildaland. One of his crew had succumbed to his injuries and was buried on the side of a hill well away from the mine. The others survived, including young Danny, who was now the main chef for the miners' boarding house in Digger's Hill.

Captain Doyle was eager to hear about his wife, Yvette. Kira watched his face beam as she told him that Mrs. Doyle was the most popular librarian amongst the children, that she was her mother's best friend, and how she had helped Kira meet the selkies. Captain Doyle did not show much emotion. He was slow to smile through the thick beard, though his sad eyes seemed to glisten from time to time. He gave the impression of a weary old man who hadn't slept in over a decade. If she ever returned home again, Kira did not want to tell Mrs. Doyle what had become of her husband; it was too depressing. She did not sleep well that night.

Back in the classroom the next day, Kira found herself longing to draw pictures of what she had heard the night before. Painting might make her feel better if she couldn't read books of fantasy. When she asked if they had paint and paintbrushes, the other children laughed. Mrs. McIver scowled at Kira and proceeded to give them all a lecture. There was no time for leisure on Hildaland, she said. Everyone had to learn a job and contribute to the community. Without hard and constant work, they would not survive on this Atlantic outpost. Furthermore, they should consider themselves fortunate they were allowed the luxury of an education, she finished with a flourish of her hands.

Still, Kira had most afternoons to herself, except for occasional skills-training sessions. She was excused from the domestic arts activities like baking, cooking, planning meals, and sewing, after having demonstrated those skills to the satisfaction of the education committee. Kira wanted to spend more time exploring the island, but found no one else who shared her curiosity or energy. Certainly no one like Cody. The other children were not unfriendly, but they had all grown up together on Hildaland and had little in common with Kira, who felt she had travelled the world in comparison. She was used to being a loner and was content to strike out on her own.

One benefit of the adults' long working hours was the lack of supervision. As long as she didn't approach the water, no one bothered Kira or seemed to care how she spent her free time. She discovered a variety of beaches, from the sandy one she had washed up on, to pebble-strewn shores, to high rock cliffs with sheer drops to the water far below. Small forests hid rabbits she loved to follow when she spotted them. Between the stands of trees were rolling grassy hills where she watched the goats bouncing off any rock outcrops they could find. They would cross a hill, one after the other like a string of beads, then turn around and go the other way. There were sheep, too, white polka dots on the emerald hills. These woollies were pretty enough, but not of much interest, since all they ever did was shuffle and eat, lie down and digest, then repeat.

In time Kira befriended some merrows who tended the livestock. She was especially fond of Jimmy, the head shepherd for the island and the only man who worked with the animals. All the others were women and older girls who sheared sheep, milked goats, and made cheese. Jimmy was unusual, Kira thought. He was gentle and shy and would rarely look people in the eye. The animals trusted him, and followed him around like a pack of pet dogs. In fact, Kira often heard him talking to the goats, who answered back like they understood each other. Perhaps it was like her conversations with the dolphins, an ability that humans did not possess.

Kira found Jimmy easy to spend time with. He didn't bother her with questions, never asked where she came from, or how she landed on the island. So she didn't ask him about his past, though she assumed he had been born and raised on Hildaland, and was perhaps in his early twenties. Jimmy preferred to be with his animals, though he didn't seem to mind Kira's company. She noticed that his voice was natural and calm when he spoke to the livestock, but he was anxious and stuttered when addressing people. One day, while they sat together on a flat hill stone overlooking the grazing sheep, she decided to ask him why he didn't work in the mine with all the other men.

"Oh, Miss Kira, I c-c-can't go underground. They sent me down one time, when I was eighteen, in this c-c-c-cage, like, and it was pitch black down there. It was awful. I w-w-was so frightened. You see, I have this c-c-condition. Called cl-cl-cl-claustrophobia. C-c-can't be in small spaces, see?" Jimmy stared at his bare feet, his entire body trembling as he recounted his terrifying experience. Kira was sorry she had asked and decided not to ask him any more personal questions.

A few days later on one of her solo outings, Kira was following a rabbit along a narrow animal track when she heard a curious sound coming from the middle of a thick patch of woods. She crept slowly toward the noise: a tinkle like a small waterfall. Her final push between two cedar bushes brought her into a rocky clearing. There it was, a tiny stream pouring into a pool at the centre.

Kira had come across other streams before, but they all ran into the sea. She wondered why this one didn't form a larger pool or lake and flow over into another rivulet to eventually drain off the island. The center of the pool was black, which meant it was very deep. She also noticed that there was seaweed growing at the edges, instead of the usual mosses and freshwater plants of other streams.

Kira dipped her cupped hand into the pool to taste the water. It was slightly salty. She knelt at the edge and put both hands into the water, spreading her fingers wide. Nothing changed. Then she plunged her arms and head all the way into the water and wiggled her fingers. Webs! Her hands had webs again, which meant salt water well below the surface. Where did it come from?

A voice in her head shouted, "Follow the salt!" and without another thought she dove in and swam down, deep into the darkness. Down into a tunnel, down, down. Kira had changed into her merrow form, her tail driving her through the column of water. As dim as it was, her sensitive eyes could still make out the rough, rocky sides of the tunnel. It began to level out and now she was swimming parallel to the ground above her.

Kira swam for at least ten minutes before she detected a faint light ahead. She slowed, though her heart raced on. When she reached the opening of the long, narrow cave, she stopped and peeked out. Several small silver fish flitted by, then a few more. Kira stuck her head out and looked up.

She could see the surface far above, and she could hear the rumble and feel the vibration of waves pounding on rock. After a few moments, she made out the form of a large, narrow fish, perhaps a shark, cruising slowly from right to left. She had to be at the rocky coast, the cliff edge of the island. Kira was down far enough that sharks or finfolk sentries likely wouldn't notice her if she remained still. She withdrew her head back into the cave. Kira had just found an escape route! Now all she needed was a plan.

Chapter Nine–
Distress Call

Long after her heart rate returned to normal, Kira continued to rest on the ledge just inside the cave entrance. She was thinking hard, considering her options. She could return to the village and let them know about this escape route. But what good was it to the humans or adult merrows who couldn't breathe underwater? Perhaps some of the merrowlings could change back, but she didn't know any well enough to trust with such a serious and tricky mission. Anyway, they probably wouldn't want to leave their parents and the only home they knew.

And she also had to weigh the risks to herself. It appeared Kira was on her own, as usual. Would she be able to make a dash for it, hoping she would not be spotted from above? And what if they had a killer whale or shark patrolling down at her level? Or worse, one of the giant squid? What about the changeling finfolk? Could she outswim them?

It was probably too risky. She wished she had more options, like morphing into a log. Then she remembered, she did have an option. Now was the time to try a dolphin distress call. But what if it attracted an orca or finfolk? If she saw any approach the cave, she'd swim back up the tunnel to the pool. One thing in her favour, the passage at the entrance was too narrow for sharks or finfolk guards to enter.

Kira puckered her lips and contracted her throat. The first attempt was weak and sounded more like a squawking chicken. She closed her eyes and concentrated, recalling the detailed instructions Steen had given her. "EEE-U-EEE-U-EEE!" This time the call sounded perfect to her ears. Steen assured her the call he taught her was very specific to his dolphin clan. Still, she was nervous, hoping it would not be picked up by the whales, who might use similar calls.

Kira waited, watching as fish swam by, but no dolphins appeared. She looked out from time to time to see if the sentry swimmers above her were still on patrol. They seemed to swim by every few minutes. How long had it been, fifteen minutes, half an hour? She decided to try another call and pursed her lips.

At that very moment, a huge dark object blocked the entrance, and Kira froze. She tried to make out what it was. She saw a white patch move past, then more black, then it had moved on and the opening was clear again. Kira crept forward to take a peek but it had returned, completely blocking her view. She flattened herself against the wall as a large eye moved across the opening then disappeared. Another flash of white, then black and it was gone. A killer whale, she thought, her heart pounding in her ears. So close. Had it seen her? She didn't budge for a long while, then decided to look out again. Nothing in view.

She didn't dare make the distress call again. Discouraged, Kira twisted around in the small space and began her way back up. She would have to try calling another time, she thought. And anyway, the dolphins could be too far away to hear her, or not be able to get through the whirlwater. It was probably a waste of her time to try again. She turned the corner and began to rise up the tunnel when she felt a tug on her tail. Kira screamed, and beat her tail hard to get away from whatever had touched her.

"It's me, Cass!"

Kira continued up a few more beats to where the tunnel widened and whipped around to face the dolphin who had followed her.

"Thank goodness! You don't know how glad I am to see you!" she sputtered.

Kira heard an odd bubbling behind Cass as they rose higher in the tunnel to where there was more room. She counted three dolphins altogether. They squeaked with excitement but Kira could not understand them.

"We couldn't come right away," Cass explained. "We weren't far off when you called, but there are so many sharks, and those whales are big trouble. We had to wait until they had cleared off before we could get to you."

Kira thanked them again, then explained her situation. She asked if they could help her get away from the island, and back to her mainland home. The dolphins huddled with their heads together, babbling in low tones. Then they turned back to her.

"Okay, here's what we propose. You go back up for now, and we'll get reinforcements. Well actually, just one reinforcement, but he is *really, really big*!" Cass emphasized, then all three giggled. "Sherman is our secret weapon. With Sherman, we don't worry about whales, or those oversized dummy sharks, or the freaky finfolk."

Kira was intrigued. "Who is Sherman? What is Sherman?"

Cass paused a moment before he replied. "You know those things people sit under when they're on the beach? Kind of like the top half of a ball, cut open, and stuck on a pole?"

Kira tried to picture what he was describing. "You mean a shade? Or umbrella?"

"Sure, if that's what you call it," Cass said. "So, Sherman is like a gigantic umbrella with eight legs. He's like magic. He can change shape and he can change colour, depending on what he is moving over."

"I remember reading about that in a science magazine! He must be an octopus who can camouflage himself. He blends in with the background. And you say he's really big? Bigger than a killer whale or a giant squid?" Kira was trying to picture Sherman, and she wondered if such an enormous octopus could possibly exist.

"He's as long as the giants, but when he spreads out, he's way bigger! And he's fast. We have a hard time keeping up with him at full speed. Don't worry, Sherman will get you out of here. Once we find him. He's a popular guy, but he's kind of shy. And when he does his camouflage thing, it's impossible to see him."

They agreed that Kira should return to her island home and come back to the pool daily to check for a message. The dolphins would bring up empty clamshells and toss them around the pool when they had found Sherman. She would then return the following morning and be ready to go.

When they had left, Kira felt abandoned and more alone than she had in a long time. She was very fond of her royal parents, but Cass and his pals were the closest things to friends she had in the underwater world. With reluctance she resurfaced and climbed out of the pool. It was already dusk as she wrung out her long hair and dried out a bit before starting for home. As she left the pool to return to the village, she made note of landmarks along the way. She did not want to forget how to find the pool.

Neither Calista nor Currin had returned from work by the time Kira slipped into the house that evening. Later, as they ate supper, her parents did not comment on how quiet Kira was. She knew they were weary from work, and had many concerns, and she feared she had become a burden on them, too. Perhaps it was just as well she was about to leave. She had already decided she would tell no one, not even her parents, about her discovery. Once she was gone, she knew they would worry, so she would leave them a note, but a better one than she had left for Mrs. Doyle.

Anyway, she expected to see Calista and Currin again. She already had bigger plans brewing. Her escape from Hildaland would be just the beginning.

Chapter Ten–
A Crowded House

Days went by, then a week, then another. There were no clamshells by the pool. There was no Cass. Kira swam down to the cave entrance several times, but there was no sign of dolphins, just fish, sharks, finfolk, and whales. She began to wonder if the dolphins had played a colossal joke on her. There was no such thing as a giant, camouflaging octopus who could swim at warp speed through the water. On several nights Kira shed a few tears, thinking again how naïve she was, disappointed that her escape plan was just a dream. Cass was simply a boastful, immature dolphin, just like so many boys she knew both on the mainland and on the island. And sure she had saved his life in the past, but his father had already repaid that favour.

The days were getting shorter, the temperature colder, her parents still dejected about the possibility that Merhaven might be lost forever. Kira didn't think things could get worse until she walked into her classroom after mid-morning break one day and saw Borin sitting in the front row, grinning at her. Her jaw dropped, her heart pounded, and she spun around and left the room. What was he doing at her school? How was it possible? She did not want to see or talk to Borin. Ever! Without a word of explanation she marched past a startled Mrs. McIver and another teacher still standing at the outside door, and ran home. To her surprise, Calista was just about to leave the house.

"Kira, why aren't you at school?"

"It's Borin," she said. "He's in my class. What's he doing there?" Kira stood in the round-topped doorway, her hands on her hips.

"Oh my," Calista said. "I just found out myself, Kira. Apparently he wasn't fitting in where he was. So they sent both of the children here when they learned Currin was related to them. They arrived this morning, just after you left for school."

"They're not staying here, are they?"

"Well, the elders of their village thought they might. We do have a larger house, Kira. We have the room."

"I don't think so!" Kira shouted. "There's not enough room for me *and* them!" And she ran out the door, down the road, and into the forest. How dare they come to live off the people they had betrayed? The nerve! Large tears of frustration and anger streamed down her cheeks.

By the time her tears had subsided, Kira found herself approaching the pool. A nice swim to cool off, she thought, that's what she needed. When she arrived she was greeted by her third surprise of the day. Clamshells! All kinds of them sprinkled around the pool's edge. She wanted to shout for joy, but clamped her hands over her mouth. Yes! She was leaving, and it was going to happen tomorrow.

Then she had a sobering thought. Was it a coincidence that Borin had shown up the same day Cass finally left her a message? Perhaps this was an elaborate trick. Kira shook her head. Who was playing the trick on whom? She was becoming paranoid. She'd read too many books with conspiracy theories and devious plots. It was just a coincidence, these things happened. Still, she was uneasy.

Kira spent the rest of the day visiting the shepherds, helping them look for two lost kid goats, and picking berries once the mischievous babies were reunited with their frantic mothers.

By the time she headed for home, she had decided to be friendly to her cousins. After all, soon she would be gone, and they would be stuck on Hildaland—for now, anyway. It annoyed her that they would be cared for by her own parents, but she tried not to think about that. She had to focus on tomorrow morning. Only that.

Her cousins seemed pleased to see Kira. They told her about how poorly they had been treated, the awful food they had to eat—which was the same type of food Kira and the villagers ate every day. They also complained that they weren't allowed to swim. They had never been on dry land before and they found it most disagreeable. As she listened to their complaints, Kira thought that they were lucky they inherited mostly merrow traits and not finfolks'. They would have been truly miserable as crocodilic monsters on land. And then everyone would have hated and complained about *them*.

Kira supposed they were still in shock from losing their status—once a prince and princess, now prisoners. When her parents were out of the room, she asked her cousins if they had heard about the finfolk takeover of Merhaven, their palace home.

"No, that's not possible!" Borin insisted. "I heard the rumours, too, but it's not true."

"How do you know it's not true?" Kira asked.

"It just isn't."

"Are you saying you know something the rest of us don't? Who told you?"

"No one, I just know!"

"And do you know your mother is finfolk?" The words slipped out before Kira could snatch them back.

"She is not!" Borin and Amelie shouted at the same time. Amelie burst into tears, and Calista rushed in.

Kira dashed off to her room while Calista tried to console her cousins. Later, when all was quiet in the house, Currin came in to see her.

"Now Kira, what you said was most unkind," he said. "They are already upset by everything that has happened to them. They are my niece and nephew, and they are not responsible for what their parents did. Do you understand what I am saying?"

Kira wanted to argue with him, but decided not to say anything. She had promised herself to behave around her cousins, and not create a stir before her escape. So she merely nodded, staring at her hands folded in her lap.

"Tomorrow," he continued, "I want you to show them around the village. I've told your teacher you will be out of school for one more day."

Kira gasped. "Tomorrow? I need to go to school tomorrow. I, I have a project to present," she lied. "I can take them around the day after. Okay? And I promise to be nice to them."

"I'd like you to take them around tomorrow. You can show them the bakery, the weavery, the goats and sheep, all the places you like to go. You are a good girl, Kira, a true princess." He kissed the top of her head and left the room.

What rotten timing, Kira thought. She had to figure out a way to get to the pool somehow. The last thing she needed was two untrustworthy, half-finfolk tagalongs. Sleep did not come easily to her that night, worried as she was about how she would manage her escape the next day.

Kira was up early, still tired but eager to get going. Calista and Currin were pleased with her enthusiastic attitude, though her cousins glowered at her. Kira ignored their looks. She led them around the village, quickly showing them the various buildings, introducing them to the youngest children who were not in school yet. Both cousins looked bored and unimpressed, and barely spoke to her.

"Let's go up to the goat sheds now," she suggested. "We can watch them milking the goats, and making cheese." Borin rolled his eyes, though Amelie showed a spark of interest.

Kira took them up the long hill to the milking sheds and introduced them to the shepherds. Amelie stared transfixed as the goats stood patiently, chewing, occasionally bleating. A young woman pulled on their teats and squirted milk into a wooden pail. Even Borin looked over once in a while, his scowl beginning to soften.

Kira slipped outside to speak to Jimmy in private. "Can you do me a big favour and take them to the creamery? I'm sure they'd love to see how cheese is made, and maybe taste a sample," she whispered. "Nature calls, I need to make a little trip into the woods."

He chuckled and nodded his head. "Take your time, M-Miss Kira."

"And please don't let them follow me," she said, hurrying off. She hoped they wouldn't miss her anytime soon. Probably they'd be delighted to be rid of her. Her cousins appeared truly offended by what she had said about their mother, so perhaps they really didn't know the truth about her. And they looked sincerely distressed that finfolk might plan to invade their underwater home.

But now she needed to focus on her new mission. Once she was amongst the trees she broke into a run, still worried her cousins might follow her. She arrived at the pool out of breath and was relieved to see the clamshells still there. Kira removed her wool pullover, kicked off her leggings and moccasins, and carefully hid them in the surrounding bushes. Then she gathered up the shells and tossed them into the center of the pool to remove all evidence of the sea. They fluttered like flower petals before sinking into the black depths. Then Kira dove in behind them.

Chapter Eleven–
Sherman

Kira swam cautiously to the cave entrance. Her unease since Borin's appearance had revved up her nervous energy; she practically buzzed with it. She wanted to be ready for anything, including a surprise attack from in front or behind.

The entrance appeared to be clear. She crept up to the edge of the opening and peeked out. She saw nothing out of the ordinary. No dolphins, no giant octopus, no orca sentries. Looking up, she spied a pair of sharks cruising away from the cliff wall. Kira prepared herself for a long wait, and hoped she hadn't already missed her escort. She didn't want to consider that possibility, but all the things that could go wrong were jamming any positive thoughts she could muster.

Kira heard a squeak and shrank back inside a little. A dolphin or a whale? A second later Cass shot into the opening, barely squeezing in beside her. Kira would have hugged him if she could move her arms. Instead, she laughed with relief.

"You made it!" she said.

"Sorry it took so long to get back here," Cass said. "Sherman was on the other side of the ocean, and the only way to find him was by messengers. Those sea turtles are reliable, but slow. Anyway, he had another job to finish first."

"Job?"

"Yeah, he hires out. Like I said before, he has some unique talents. And we've got real troublemakers undersea. You wouldn't believe some of the battles that go on. Anyway, we're on the clock, as you humans say—"

"I'm not a human," Kira corrected him.

"Of course, sorry," he apologized. "But at times you merrows act like humans. Maybe not as violent or greedy. These killer whales, though, they're like the worst of the humans. And that's what's holding us up. There's a big one in this area, and I think he's got his eye on this cave."

"Yeah, I saw that eye the first time I came down here. And he probably saw mine."

"That was him. Big fella. We had to wait until he was gone before we could get to you. So I came alone this time. With Sherman, of course. The fewer of us the better."

Kira shuddered.

"I know what you're thinking, Kira," Cass said in a soothing voice. "I can feel how anxious you are. Here's what we're going to do. Sherman will give the signal when all is clear. Then I will go out first, and you right behind me. Stay close enough that you can touch me with your arms. Got that?"

"Uh-huh."

"You won't recognize Sherman. Just trust me and stay right behind me, no matter what you see or think you see. Sherman will be in one of his usual crazy disguises."

"As what?"

"Well, right now he's lying on the bottom disguised as a flat boulder. Soon he's coming up to get us. As a killer whale."

"A what?"

"Kira, it's the only thing he can be that will hide you from anyone above us and that won't stir up suspicion. We'll swim beside or under him until we're out of the area. Then he'll switch into whatever works best as we go. That's how he does it."

Kira stared at Cass's eyes, a few inches from her face. Could she be certain this was Cass, and not a finfolk in disguise? She didn't know if finfolk could mimic dolphins, but there was a lot she didn't know about changeling creatures, including her own merrow folk.

She had two options at that moment. To return to the drudgery of life on Hildaland, a prisoner forever, or to take a chance she might be eaten by an orca. She studied his eyes again, large and earnest. How could any finfolk mimic those soulful eyes?

"Okay," she said, and swallowed. "I'm ready."

The minutes that followed were the longest in her life. Was she about to embark on freedom, or death?

Kira felt a slight vibration in the cave wall. "Is that the signal?" she asked in a whisper.

"No," Cass whispered back. "That was a warning to wait."

Then the cave darkened as a black object blocked the light coming in. Both Kira and Cass flattened themselves against the walls as best as they could. "Close your eyes," he whispered.

Kira shut her eyes. A moment passed. "You can open them again."

"Why did I have to close my eyes?"

"Because if you make eye contact, the whale will know you're in here and alive."

Kira trembled a little but said nothing more. A few minutes later, there was a more pronounced vibration in the walls.

"That's our signal."

"Are you sure?"

"Yes. Get ready!"

Once again, the cave darkened, and this time Kira felt Cass slip out and away from her. Before panic overwhelmed her she launched herself out of the opening. Outside there was enough light that Kira could just see Cass in front of her. He seemed to attach himself to the side of the great black hulk lumbering past them, like a parasite fastened to a fish. Kira latched on just behind him, but kept beating her tail. As the great black creature began to swing away from the rock face of the island, Cass started to swim under him, and Kira followed. She could make out white markings on the side, just like the killer whale she'd seen. She gulped. He looked *exactly* like an orca.

As they approached the seabed, Cass slid back and positioned himself alongside Kira. "Look straight ahead," he said.

Another killer whale was approaching them. Maybe the sentry they'd seen earlier.

"Uh-oh. Now what?"

"I don't know," Cass replied. "Sherman can look like a whale, but he can't communicate in their language."

"Can you?" Kira asked.

"Nah, they'd catch on, they're too smart for that. Don't worry. Sherman will figure something out. Just be ready to move fast, and whatever you do, stay under him!"

They heard a deep boom from the killer whale who swam out of sight for a moment. Sherman suddenly zoomed forward at an amazing speed and it was all Kira could do to keep up with him. He swam up, then almost straight down. Next a sharp left, then right, then down again. Kira and Cass were hurtling toward the sea floor like torpedoes, and she felt a scream starting to form in her throat, certain they would be crushed under Sherman's weight once they hit bottom. But just as they almost touched the sand, he came to a full stop, as if he had landed on a solid surface.

Kira and Cass settled on the sand, staring at each other, with Sherman just inches above them. They heard more booms, low creaks, and whines, but Sherman did not move. He had become a house-sized rock, hovering over them.

Once the orca calls had stopped, Kira whispered, "Now what?"

"Sherman will know when it's safe to move again. Be patient. He must be disguised as the sea floor right now. Anyway, he needs to rest once in a while, too. All those evasive manoeuvres take a lot of fuel."

"Yeah, as long as he doesn't forget we're here."

"Don't worry, Kira. Sherman's gotta be the smartest creature on this planet. He's a floating encyclopedia. At least I think that's what you'd call it in your schools."

Kira nodded, impressed.

"And he's been around a long, long time. Centuries, they say. He's a history book, too."

"I thought octopuses didn't live very long."

"Uh, Sherman is not an ordinary octopus."

Kira closed her eyes and laid her head on the soft sand. They needed a few Shermans on land, too, she thought, as she drifted off to sleep under the biggest umbrella in the sea.

Kira was awakened by a bump, Cass's nose on her forehead. She opened her eyes in surprise to see a fish in his mouth.

"Hunfy?"

"What?" she asked.

"Fif. Eat," he said and bobbed his head around to make the fish flop.

"Oh, food, fish, eat, got it. Was I asleep?"

Cass dropped the fish in front of her and Kira, finally aware of her keen hunger, ate the whole thing nose to tail.

"You slept like a clam," he said. "Guess you were tired."

"Yeah," she said. "I didn't get much sleep last night, worrying about how to get to the pool on time. And without company."

Cass made a whining noise, and the huge mass above them rumbled.

"Are we starting up again? He sounds like a gigantic ship engine."

"Yup, we're heading off. We're just outside their fog zone, so we still need to be careful. Ready to swim?"

Kira nodded her head and Cass whined again, at a higher pitch. Sherman started slowly then picked up speed. He rose up off the floor so they had more room to move and stretch, and the pace was perfect for Kira. She now had the luxury of studying all the bottom-dwelling creatures, which she didn't the other times she'd passed through these waters. The variety of starfish surprised her, as well as the different crabs and flatfish. The seaweeds were also different from the ones nearer to her home. Some formed large tree-like branches, and others resembled fuzzy round bushes or lichens.

"Ah, loram puffs!" she cried and plucked a few as she swam by, popping them into her mouth as if she'd been eating them all her life. "Care to try them?" she asked Cass, who shook his head.

"I'm a carnivore," he said, and laughed at the look on her face. "Meat only for me. You omnivores will eat nearly anything. Yuck."

They continued to move close to the bottom of the sea for a long time, stopping often to rest and to eat. When Kira asked Cass if Sherman needed to eat, he told her that the big octopus had prepared for this journey by first having a very large meal.

"What does he eat?" she asked.

"Whatever he can catch," Cass said, and began rolling and nodding his head and jerking his body like he was having convulsions. When he finished his laughing fit, he looked Kira in the eye and said, "You don't want to know."

For a moment Kira was alarmed. "You're such a worrier, Kira. He doesn't eat humans or merrows or dolphins or even seals. Their fur is too ticklish. But most anything else he can fit into his big stretchy mouth is game. I think he particularly likes sharks, barracudas, stuff like that."

"How about small orcas or finfolk?" Kira asked.

"Mmm, maybe. Finfolk might be a bit prickly. They like to wear metal. Probably give him indigestion."

Cass was right, she really didn't want to know any more about Sherman's eating habits.

"I have one more question for you, Cass. How did you get through the whirlwater at their border? How did we do it with Sherman?"

Cass seemed to shiver for a moment. "Oh, yeah, love the whirlwater, what a blast! We dolphins like to ride them around and around till we can't count anymore, then we shoot out. It's so fast you can't tell if you're being ejected or sucked in." He wiggled with pleasure. "I don't know what Sherman does, I think he just charges through. Didn't feel a thing, did you?"

"No. Nothing like my solo trip through to Hildaland on the surface." Kira was already thinking about how she might return with reinforcements.

To Kira, with no way to mark time, it felt like they had travelled at least two days when they finally reached the dolphin rendezvous. Only then was she formally introduced to Sherman, facing him eye to enormous eye. Her heart raced wildly with excitement and some alarm when she realized her entire body was the size of his eyeball. Although she was unable to communicate with him, Cass translated for her. She wanted to know how she could repay Sherman for his services.

"He says getting you out of that prison was payment enough for him. But, if you wish to please him further, he would like to see the others on Hildaland freed. He can't do it alone. Besides, they have to be rescued from dry land."

Kira smiled at that request. "Tell him that is exactly what I intend to do once I return home. And also, tell him I am forever grateful to him and I hope I'll see him again."

When Cass's father Steen and the rest of their pod arrived at the rendezvous place, Sherman put on a farewell display for them. First he turned a brilliant red, then he grew bright yellow spots, which were followed by green stripes on deep purple. He waved his suckered legs in a hypnotic rhythm as fluorescent spots flickered on and off around his eyes and on top of his large domed head. Then, the most amazing trick of all, he simply vanished. One minute he was dancing above them, the next moment he was gone.

The pod was performing their own dance of joy,

darting this way and that, bobbing up and down, squeaking, buzzing, and clicking as they played. Kira was still staring at the spot where Sherman had been, and noticed a faint ripple in the hue of the water. Aha, she thought, not only could Sherman mimic and blend into the solid objects nearby, he could turn into the colour of the sea around him. What a talented octopus. And a kind, generous one, too, who worked for peace in the sea world. Cody was going to love this!

The last leg of Kira's trip was much shorter. The dolphin pod stayed with her until she was very near the shore of her home village. As they approached, Kira swam up to Cass and tapped him on a flipper.

"Cass, I want to thank you and your friends for all the risks you took to help me escape. And I'm sorry if I got you into trouble with your dad. I know he didn't want you to get so close to Hildaland."

A succession of bubbles burst out of Cass's blowhole and he rolled several times before he answered. "Dad and I worked it out. I'm old enough now to make those decisions, and, anyway, I know he's proud of me. Of course, if I went in there just to tease the orcas and finfolk, he wouldn't be so happy." His head bobbed. "But helping a princess escape from slavery? My pleasure entirely, Your Highness." Cass bowed his head, made a large circle, and shot to the surface for air.

When the pod finally stopped at the cove south of

the village harbour, Kira was felt both relief and sadness. What if she never saw them again? She asked Steen what she could do to repay them for their kindness.

"We've become very fond of you, Princess Kira," Steen said.

Kira blushed to hear herself addressed this way.

"You are an uncommon merrow, and a credit to your kind. But if you choose to live on land with the humans, we would be most grateful if you could teach the fishermen to watch for us when they fish. If they must fish on a grand scale, they could use nets that don't harm dolphins. Also, discourage them from capturing us and keeping us in prisons for display and entertainment."

Kira nodded. She knew how difficult this would be, but she intended to do her best to help her friends and dolphins everywhere.

"May I still call on you?" she asked, worried that they had already spent so much time and effort to keep her safe. "But only if it's really important," she added.

"Of course, Princess. You know how to find us. Farewell until our next encounter," Steen said, and with that the pod turned as one, and swam off.

Kira's sadness suddenly evaporated and she smiled. Yes, there would be another encounter—she could feel it in the look Steen had given her. And she knew she'd be returning to Hildaland at least one more time.

Chapter Twelve–
Gathering Forces

When Kira's head broke through to the surface, she knew difficult challenges still awaited her. The seas were rough, the wind sharp and cold. She'd lost track of time on Hildaland; it could be the middle of December, or perhaps Christmas had come and gone already—she had no idea. This was much worse than the first time she'd taken a non-parent-authorized undersea field trip a few months earlier. But at least, once again, she had made it back again all in one piece. Only her mind was still in turmoil.

She pushed herself onto the shore of the small selkie cove and ran to the boulders, where she prayed she'd find her clothes and a working cell phone. Luck was with her as she pulled on her jacket and boots, gasping and shivering violently. It helped that Mrs. Doyle had given her the latest K model cell with a graphene battery. Even so, only one bar of energy was left on the cell, and her hand shook as she began punching in the numbers for her ride home. She knew her parents must have been sick with worry all these weeks, but first she had to contact the person she'd promised to call if there was trouble.

"Mrs. Doyle?" she asked when the phone was picked up at the other end.

"Kira! Is that you? Where *are* you?" Yvette Doyle's hysterical voice was barely recognizable to Kira's ears.

"I'm back at the cove, Mrs. Doyle. Can you give me a ride home?"

"Are you okay? Are you alone?"

"I'm fine, just a little cold. I can wait for you by the road."

Kira heard Mrs. Doyle panting like she was out of breath. "Okay, stay just off the road, I'll know exactly where to find—" The phone went dead.

Kira was soon settled back at home after giving a full account of her adventures to her parents and Mrs. Doyle. The librarian leaked tears the entire time, with Bess's arm around her quivering shoulders. She stifled a sob upon first hearing that her husband was still alive. Kira left out the details of his sad appearance and broken demeanour.

Before Kira went to bed that evening, though it was very late, she had to call Cody.

"Oh man, Kira, you had us so worried. I mean, I know you can take care of yourself, but that was a long time. You missed Christmas. Did you celebrate with your merrow family?" He was gasping, as if he'd just run a race. Kira could picture him pacing around his house as he talked, his free arm waving like a flapping flag in a windstorm.

"No, I didn't know it was Christmas last week. I guess they don't do Christmas. Every day is the same. Time is different there, somehow. Maybe it goes faster. Their weeks are only six days long."

"Huh? That doesn't make sense. Never mind, you're probably tired. We can catch up tomorrow, if that's okay with you. We don't go back to school until the day after."

In spite of her exhaustion and her anxiety about what lay ahead, Kira smiled as she pulled the covers up to her chin. The people she cared for the most were all grownups except for Cody. And he was acting and sounding like an adult more and more. An unusual boy, he was thoughtful, serious, responsible. But best of all, he was a loyal friend who listened to and believed in her. He was her collaborator.

Kira did have a pang of regret when she remembered she had not left a note for Currin and Calista. She'd done it again! She was so worried about her cousins' arrival and how to get away from them, she'd completely forgotten the promise she'd made to herself. Her poor parents, saddled with two whining kids, and now their found daughter was lost again. But she intended to make it up to them.

The news of Hildaland and the prisoners caused

a great deal of distress as well as hope within the merrow community and their human families. However, the shock wore off eventually, and within days they were discussing plans on how to mount a rescue. There were many details and difficulties to overcome. First, how to find the island. No free human had ever seen it. Second, how would they land? Kira said as far as she knew there were no wharves or docks to tie up to, so they'd need smaller boats like fishing dories to get on shore. Finally, who would go? They surely would need several large boats to take all the people back, plus bring food and supplies if they had to leave any behind for a while.

There were other concerns as well. Would they need weapons against the finfolk on land? Kira had never seen the silver mine or the community of Digger's Hill. She had no idea how the labourers were guarded and controlled. Currin had been reluctant to talk about those things. Would they need protection from attack by sea? They didn't worry so much about sharks, but the large finfolk could create problems for them from below by sabotaging the boats. Would the killer whales interfere? What about giant squid?

It was decided they should hold off the rescue operation until after the winter storms had passed. That gave them time to organize the boats and people who would be part of the force. Kira's parents located the volunteers willing to help. They asked people in other villages up and down the eastern shore who knew about merrows, many of whom were married to them. Most landed merrows like her mother were eager to be included. All the fishing communities had missing, unrecovered relatives who had either drowned, or may have been captured and imprisoned on Hildaland.

As the news spread up and down the coast, the first to step forward and volunteer was Curtis Morgan. He was a renowned dory builder from a large town about an hour's drive north. Curtis was also a union labour leader, committed to helping others, and well-connected in the fishing communities. The moment this tall, broad-shouldered man stepped into their home, Kira knew he was a merrow. He had the greenest eyes she had ever seen, and he wore his long, russet hair tied back in a bushy ponytail.

He gripped her father's hand and slapped him on the back. "By Neptune, it's good to see you, Cillian Cox! Been much too long, eh? And here's our lovely Bessabel!" he said as he kissed the top of her head. "Sorry, I mean Bess," he corrected himself and gave Kira a sheepish glance.

"And you are our own Princess Kira," he said, and bowed his head, his emerald eyes twinkling. "It's an honour to meet such a brave and big-hearted lass. A credit to our merrow folk, you are. I am here at your service!" he boomed and broke into a loud, delighted laugh. They all laughed with him; he was irresistible. Kira blushed and giggled.

Kira's parents had prepared a hearty lunch for their guest and a few local friends who dropped in to meet Curtis. Among them was Fred Gimli, a fisherman, and his wife, Cyndi, both close family friends from their village. Kira had recently learned that Cyndi was also a mermaid. In a short span of time it had become clear to Kira that there were many secret merrows who had adopted land life. They blended in well, unrecognized by most of the humans around them. Cody was the one exception. He had created a list of suspected landed merrows, all of which had been confirmed by Bess.

While the adults organized themselves and the parts they would play in the rescue, Kira's job was to marshal the underwater contingent. She was certain the dolphins would be happy to help her. They also had something to gain by helping to rescue humans. If they were successful, the fishermen would owe a debt to the dolphins. Kira planned to keep her promise to help protect the dolphins from fishing nets and capture.

Then, of course, there was Sherman. If only there were several Shermans, Kira thought. If only he could come up on land, fly through the air. She could dream. But she was also aware that Sherman's magic tricks were based on his biological nature. He was a true force to be reckoned with.

She tried to imagine the scene when they landed on Hildaland, how happy everyone would be to know they were free again. Her royal parents would be so proud of her. Then the image of Borin and Amelie tagging along behind them spoiled the vision. Still, since she'd returned to her adoptive parents, Kira did not have the same sour feelings about her cousins as when they'd arrived in Noville. She realized she'd been jealous of them. First because they had lived in the palace where she and her royal parents should have reigned, then for interrupting the life she had started with her new family on Hildaland.

Now, safe on her mainland home, she felt sorry for Borin and Amelie. They were neither merrow nor finfolk. If their true parentage were discovered, they could be rejected by both sides. The finfolk probably knew already, so her cousins were treated like all the other captives on the island. Once the merrows and humans found out, well, they would be bullied and called freaks, at least by other children if not by the adults. But for now she concentrated on the huge task ahead. As Kira's mother had said, they still had a lot of work to do before anyone was going to be freed.

Chapter Thirteen–
Lost and Found

Long before spring, the communities along Kira's stretch of coastline were buzzing with anticipation, anxious to begin Operation LASTCAF (Lost at sea, then captured and freed). When the day before the start of the mission finally came, the excitement had died to a sombre simmer. Seven large boats were tied up at the wharf, each manned by crews of four to six people. Voices were low and serious as the last of the supplies were stowed. This was the most unusual and serious fishing trip any of them had ever embarked on.

Kira was delighted that Cody was coming along. The two of them would travel in the lead ship, skippered by her father. The day before they launched, a proud Cillian Cox gave them a tour. "This fine vessel, *Saving Grace*, belongs to Marcus Graham. He owns the cannery in Greyling Bay. His two younger brothers were lost at sea many years ago. Marcus knows there's no guarantee that his brothers will be found on Hildaland, but as you know he's willing to send his ship and finance the trip to help any others."

He pointed to the two dories lined up end to end on the top deck. "There's a couple of punts down below, too. And wait till you see the fancy captain's chair. She's got the most modern navigational and safety equipment available. Sonar, radar, the whole works. For a big girl, she glides through the water like a knife slides through pudding."

Kira's father had such a dreamy look on his bearded face, she tried not to giggle at the picture of a boat plowing through vanilla pudding.

"C'mon below, I'll show you all the gauges, screens, bells, and whistles. It'll pop the brains out your ears. But don't worry, I've taken her out a few times, it's all really simple if you know your way around a boat."

The seven vessels pushed off without noise or fuss into the darkness and calm seas of early morning. Kira was still somewhat anxious that they might not find Hildaland. So much depended on her underwater guides. She had already conversed with Steen before she boarded the ship that morning.

"The pod is ready, Kira," he assured her. "Two dolphins per vessel, with three scouts leading the way, and two at the rear of the last ship. We'll provide regular reports to your onboard merrows. You should have plenty of warning if there is trouble ahead." He chuckled. "I believe you are familiar with the advance guard. They have made this journey before."

"Cass and his friends?" Kira smiled when Steen nodded his head and twirled in the water. She guessed he was proud of his brave and clever son but might not admit it.

Each boat had at least one merrow on board to communicate with dolphins. They did not wish to leave anything to chance in case the boats lost contact with each other. Bess was one of those merrows. Cyndi had also wished to join their forces, but since her husband, Fred, insisted on going, she needed to stay home with their four youngsters. Both Fred and Curtis were sailing on *Saving Grace* along with Cody, Kira, her father, and one other fisherman.

Except for Curtis, Kira had never met the merrows who came from neighbouring villages and towns along the coast. But she'd become adept at spotting them: the large eyes, slightly larger hands, and a subtly different way of walking.

"I wonder if the children who have one merrow and one human parent can change to merrows in salt water," Cody mused while they stood on the deck of the boat on that first day of their voyage. "Maybe they'd like to participate in science experiments when we get back," he said, grinning at Kira.

"Not if their mothers are like mine," Kira warned him.

"Good point," he agreed. "You probably won't believe how scared I was of your mom after you disappeared again. I mean, she knew I had to be involved somehow. I was thinking I'd rather face a mother grizzly bear."

"She's not *that* bad!"

"No, she was pretty cool about it the first time. Still, I felt bad when they found out you were really gone this time, and I knew what you were up to. Your mom took it pretty hard. Then my mom took it out on me." Cody grimaced.

"Yeah, sorry about that. But Mrs. Doyle confessed. You weren't really involved, nobody should have been mad at you."

"I guess my mom thought I should have stopped you. As if I could. Anyway, it's okay. You came back."

"And now I'm returning. I hope this rescue is going to work. And I hope that ammunition you researched will do the job," Kira said, worried again.

"Well, if it doesn't, you can always outrun the finfolk or climb up trees."

"Maybe," Kira said. "And what if they have weapons we don't know about?"

"They probably would have used them by now. Your merrow parents would have told you, wouldn't they?"

"I suppose so."

The rescue party had decided ahead of time to sail through the night. There were enough crew members on each boat to keep them going nonstop. The dolphins also spelled each other off, though they all continued to swim. They would lead the fleet through the ring of fog around Hildaland, but would not go beyond it. Even so, no one was certain exactly how far out the shark and killer-whale sentries patrolled. Only Cass and his two friends had penetrated the guarded zone, and only because they had dared each other to answer Kira's distress call.

By the end of the second full day of sailing, a fog bank was spotted ahead of them. The setting sun turned the heavy mist a glowing orange, as if the sea were on fire. On first sight, knowing what waited for them on the other side, Kira shivered and her teeth began to chatter. She was not feeling particularly brave or smart at that moment.

Her father radioed all ships to cut engines and drop anchors. "We'll stop for the night and allow the dolphins to rest. Everybody, have a good meal and try to get a good night's sleep."

But Kira could barely sleep that night. They were so close now. She hoped their boats were not spotted out here beyond the fog ring, and that, if they were, their presence did not arouse any suspicion. For all anyone knew, they were just fishing.

At daybreak, the boats began to quietly drift into the thick, white fog, and within seconds lost sight of each other. Immediately, all navigational equipment went berserk. The gauges and dials indicated the boats were sinking. Horns began to blow, and warning messages blared out.

"Curtis!" Cillian shouted. "Looks like we're taking on water! We must have hit something! Prepare to launch dories!"

Curtis's muffled voice came from the engine room. "There's no water here! We're not sinking, the gauges are wrong!"

Dolphins and merrows were frantically receiving messages and relaying them to captains. "Ignore the instruments!" they shouted over the horns and loud-speakers. "We are not sinking! There are no shoals below, plenty of clearance! Stay the course, straight ahead!"

The crews dashed around trying to silence the auto-mated sirens and speakers, but it was too late. After all their precautions, they had announced their arrival with great fanfare.

Eventually all the warning systems were disabled and only the squeaks of dolphins and muffled shouts of merrows could be heard. Occasionally echoes from the other ships bounced through the fog and con-fused dolphins, merrows, and crew alike. Kira was especially stressed, hanging over the bow, hoping she was interpreting and repeating what she heard correctly. The thick mist was suffocating and her head felt like it would explode from built-up pressure. How could they still be in the fog? It seemed like hours had passed since they first entered the murky white soup. What if they were trapped inside the ring and simply following it around the island?

In fact, it was no longer than fifteen minutes before they finally broke through into a sunny day on the other side. Ahead of them loomed the rocky, foreboding island. The shape reminded her of a worn-down volcano she'd seen in photos, with grass-covered hills interspersed with rock cliffs at the base. Now that she was wearing her glasses, she could see the island clearly for the first time.

Curtis came up on deck to watch with Kira and Cody as they approached Hildaland, no longer hidden in the mists. "So what happened back there?" Cody asked. "Do you know why the instruments went wonky like that?"

Curtis shook his head and shrugged. "Finfolk magic, I suppose. They've been able to protect this island for ages. Hundreds of years. I'll wager it was some kind of electromagnetic force that messed up all the fancy ship electronics. I'd love to get my hands on that technology. Who knows what else we'll find when we land." He laughed heartily and rubbed his hands together.

Kira hadn't seen any sign of technology on the island, although she had never visited Digger's Hill or been anywhere near the mining area. She wondered what else she didn't know about the place. She wondered if, in spite of all their research and what she had learned while living on Hildaland, they were properly prepared to face down the finfolk. Armed with toy guns against mother grizzlies protecting their greatest love: treasures of silver.

Chapter Fifteen–
Storming Hildaland

Twenty minutes after clearing the fog ring, the ships dropped anchor and began to lower dories. They quickly filled with crews, leaving each captain and one crew member with the ships. Before Kira climbed over into a dory, her father handed her the same weapon they all carried, except for three men who also brought hand guns. She slung the water-gun strap over her shoulder. "Be careful, my daughter. If the finfolk recognize who you are, they may target you."

"I doubt it, Dad. You worry too much." She gave him a quick kiss on the cheek and climbed down into the dory with Curtis, Fred, and Cody.

There were no dolphins now to guide or warn them as they rowed toward shore. They all scanned the waters for fins, but saw nothing beyond the waves and currents carrying them in toward the rocky beaches. Kira did not recognize the shore ahead, but then she had not explored the entire island coastline.

Suddenly their dory rocked violently, first to one side, then the next. A killer whale breached just in front of the dory, washing a huge wave of water over them. Kira grabbed at a horn hanging from her neck and blew as hard as she could. It made a low, mournful howl, like a baying hound.

A huge black whale erupted out of the water beside the boat, poised to crash on top of them. Kira and Cody screamed just as a thick, snake-like coil shot out of the water and wrapped around the whale, jerking it back under. Then just as suddenly, the whale rocketed out of the water ahead of them and landed high on the rocky shore. It flapped and writhed, stranded, unable to return to the water.

"Go, Sherman!" Cody yelled, his fist pumping in the air.

Kira heard more screams and shouts from the other boats. The water all around them boiled with activity. Crews struggled to keep their dories upright, while smashing their oars on the sharks and whales that now surrounded the boats. Sharks and whales flew through the air as they were flung against the rocks on shore. Some slipped back into the water, and others remained still and broken on the beach. Bodies were piling up.

Then Kira heard a familiar voice calling, "Keep going straight. Go to the beach. All clear!"

It was Cass! Crazy Cass had come with them in spite of orders from Steen to stay back.

"Go forward!" Kira shouted to the crews, standing up in the rocking dory. "The water is clear now. Keep going!"

One by one the boats beached and the crews jumped out, avoiding the stranded sharks and whales, some still gnashing their teeth. As they started to climb up the beach, Kira's mother caught up to her and gave her a hug. Her face was grim. "Let's go find your parents, and the others."

They raced up the hill and tried to orient themselves. Kira was distracted by her mother's words. She couldn't help but wonder what her mother was feeling. Was she worried that Kira would want to live with her royal parents? Did she care? Somehow, she thought her mother did care very much, but would not let on. After all, this was also her mother's king and queen.

After a bit of wandering, Kira thought she recognized the back of the shepherds' hill. When she heard a bleating goat, she knew exactly where they were. They moved along a series of sand dunes separated by strips of tall, dead grasses and dry shrubs to get to the village. Finally, Kira saw the beach where she had washed up. There was the tree she had climbed to escape her finfolk captors.

"This way!" she shouted, and they ran toward the village. But before they reached it, Kira knew something was amiss. The normal sounds were not there. The sounds of people at work, talking, children's shouts and laughter. All was silent except for the rescue party tromping up the street.

There was no sign of life in the village. It was abandoned and totally, eerily silent. Kira ran into the house where she'd lived for nearly two months. There were bowls and utensils scattered, food left out. Someone behind her voiced her thoughts.

"Looks like they left in a hurry. Where would they go? Where were they taken?"

Kira tried not to panic. She gripped the gun strapped to her shoulder. How could they be sure these guns would work against the crocodilian monsters? She looked over at Cody and prayed that he was right, that his research was based on facts and not some writer's fancy. So far most of what they had read was very close to the truth.

Bess finally spoke. "Kira said there are about four hundred people on the island, according to King Currin. Is there a building or place large enough to hold all of them?"

Kira tried to remember everything she'd learned about Digger's Hill. Borin had boasted about the meeting hall, but it would only hold fifty people at most. Then she remembered Currin describing the caverns below the earth, places that had been scooped out and emptied of silver ore over the centuries.

"The mine!" she cried. "They have huge rooms below the earth. I'm sure they would hold that many people and more."

Curtis, in charge of the landed rescue party, unfolded one of the maps Kira had sketched for them and laid it on the table. "We're here, right?"

Kira nodded.

"Okay, we follow this path to get to the mine, or this one here. Or we can go directly to the other village. Let's split up into three groups and meet at the mine."

Curtis organized the groups, each with a leader and a map based on Kira's descriptions. "Everyone have their headlamps and flashlights ready and working?"

They all responded with clicks and flashes as they tested their equipment.

"Guns ready and loaded? Remember, no one fires unless it's necessary. Let's go!"

Kira's group started up the side of the hill next to the sheep pastures. She walked behind Fred, her group leader, and Cody followed her. The climb was familiar to Kira; it was the one that Currin took every day he went off to work. But he had never encouraged her to visit the mine. It was dirty and dangerous, he'd said, no place for children. Kira wasn't even curious about the deep, dark pits where the miners worked, buried for hours at a time. Not even to take a quick trip to look at Digger's Hill. She recalled the terrified expression on Jimmy's face when he'd described being in the mine.

The baaing of sheep and bleating of goats reminded Kira that the animals were all alone without any shepherds on the hillside. She dashed off to meet a couple of goat kids that had broken away from the flock. "I'll be right back," she called out to Fred. "I'll be just a minute," she assured him. "You'll be able to see me."

These were the same kids she had helped to round up on occasion, and they seemed to remember her. "Hey, you two, you'd better get back to your momma. There's no one to find you if you get lost now." Kira looked up at the milking shed, remembering how she had managed to get away from Borin and Amelie. Then she noticed movement through one of the open windows. She crouched low, encouraging the kids to come near her. Her heart pounded as she slowly raised her gun.

"Kira! What's going on? We need to get going," Fred shouted.

A figure emerged from the milking shed. It was Jimmy, holding his cap in his hands, looking uncertain. Kira stood up and let her gun hang loose again.

"Jimmy? Is that you?" Kira was still a little worried that he might be a finfolk in a shepherd's disguise.

"M-Miss Kira?" he said and came forward. Before he reached her, Fred was by Kira's side, his hand on a real gun.

"It's Jimmy, the shepherd," she explained, standing

in front of Jimmy, who trembled with anxiety. "He's a friend."

Fred asked him what had happened, but Jimmy stood with his mouth open, staring at Kira.

"It's okay, Jimmy," she encouraged him. "We brought a rescue party, we want to help you."

"I-I was in the w-woods," Jimmy finally said, "looking for the k-kid goats again, when all the villagers c-came through, herded by more f-f-finfolk than I'd ever seen b-before. And they were angry. I-I thought they m-might be heading for the m-m-mine. I-I d-don't like the m-mine, so I stayed in the w-woods. B-b-but if you go there, they m-might ambush you. I-I know the path to the mine, and p-places where f-f-finfolk could be hiding. I-I can show you."

Fred accepted his offer and the group continued with Jimmy in the lead. Where the woods were thick, the path narrowed and they had to walk single file, ever alert for an attack. The path then widened again onto rocky hillsides where it was easier to see all around.

"N-not much farther now," Jimmy said after forty minutes or so.

They first saw the mine from some distance away. A few wood and rock buildings stood on a plateau over-looking the sea. They had reached the opposite end of the island. The wind was strong on the north side of the volcano, blowing chilled air up off the water on this early spring day. Even so, the sun shone brightly. Kira could see the fog bank encircling the island like a fuzzy woollen collar, but their seven boats were not visible from where she stood.

By the time they reached the buildings that marked the entrances to the mine, the other two groups had already arrived. They milled about, trying to figure out how to enter the mine without using the lift. The cage held up to eight people, so they would be at the mercy of anyone waiting for them at the bottom. Jimmy wouldn't even look at the cage.

Kira wandered to the edge of the plateau and looked down at the village, Digger's Hill. It was more drab than Noville, though it contained several much larger structures. The building next to the shore that butted up against the side of the hill had to be the smelter. A tall smoke stack jutted up from one end, faint fumes wafting from the top. Currin had told her that once the ore tumbled down chutes to the smelter, it was heated to such high temperatures it would melt. Then they could separate the pure silver from the rest of the rock. The liquid silver was poured into moulds, cooled to solid metal, then taken off the island. Currin said there was an underwater exit inside the smelter. The silver bricks were dropped into this opening and then taken to wherever the finfolk stored their treasures. He believed they had another location where they turned the silver into useful or decorative items, like silver caps for their sharp teeth.

As Kira stared down at the smelter, she noticed movement in the water next to it. Even with her glasses, it was a blur, but there appeared to be a plume of a lighter colour in the water, leading away from the island.

"Cody!" she called out and was startled to see him already standing next to her. She wondered how long he'd been there. "What do you see next to the smelter, that building down there?"

"Looks like the sea bottom is being stirred up, as if something was being dragged away. Something big and heavy, I'd say."

"And I'd say it's time to get down there," Kira said.

They were finally moving in on their quarry.

Chapter Sixteen–
Island Dungeons

"Listen up, folks!" Curtis shouted from the top of a small shed. "We just compared notes, and according to our sharp-eyed trackers, it looks like our people were heading for the village down below. There's no sign they were up here or went down the shaft in the lift. So we're going to head down now, and please be very cautious. The finfolk could be hiding anywhere. Any questions?"

Kira raised her hand. "Cody and I think they might be moving something out of the smelter, underwater. We should probably check out that building," she said, pointing.

"Good work. Okay, two groups. You folks check out the village. The rest of us will head straight for the smelter."

They hurried down off the plateau, a rather steep drop, and it took very little time before they were creeping around the silent village and confirming that there wasn't a single person to be found anywhere.

The smelter, a large rectangular building made of chiselled and cemented rock bricks attached to the side of the old volcano, proved to be more difficult to investigate. All the doors were bolted shut and the windows were barred with rusted metal rods. Several of the men had brought small tools with them, and soon they were prying the bars away from the windows. The panes seemed to be made of a plastic material. All the windows were different; it appeared they had been scavenged from various places and then recycled into the building.

Within minutes three of the most slender men had climbed in through a window. After a few anxious moments they heard shouting from around the corner, where the men had managed to open one of the doors from the inside. Curtis led several others into the building to begin a thorough search. They emerged after fifteen minutes without finding any of the prisoners. Every room had been carefully searched, they said.

"Can Kira and I go inside to have a look around?" Cody asked.

"Sure," Curtis agreed, "but only if you stay close to us."

Fred nodded his approval and he and Curtis accompanied them inside the dark and drafty building. It reminded Kira of a warehouse where they overwintered boats on the mainland. They walked into a room where cauldrons were still hot and smoking: the smelting chamber. Someone had been working there not long ago, melting down the ore and purifying the silver. The smelting room was carved out of the rock face that the building backed onto. The great stack carried the smoke from the fires high up into the air over the island, creating plumes of gases like the original volcano of long ago.

Kira kept looking at the floor of the room, wondering where the sea exit was. She thought of the one in the pool on the other side of the mountain that had led to her own exit from the island. They walked into an adjoining room where they found racks of square moulds, emptied of their cooled, solidified silver bars.

"I can hear water running," Kira said. "Listen."

They all froze in place and remained silent. It was difficult to locate the source of the noise. Kira knelt down and put her ear to the ground. "I think it's under us."

"I can hear water running behind this wall," Cody said, his ear plastered to the cold, sweating rock.

Curtis, who had been feeling the wall with his fingers, also pressed his ear against it. "They're in there, I hear voices," he said quietly. "Our people. There has to be a way in."

All four of them began to examine the wall, their headlamps illuminating all the cracks and crevices in the chiselled rock face.

"Hey! Over here," Fred called out to them. He was tracing a smooth semicircle in the wall with his fingers. It was about five feet high by four feet across. "It's the finest seam I've ever seen in rock. How did they do that without tools?"

Curtis gave a dry laugh. "Our folk believe the ancients first lived on this island, before the finfolk turned it into a work colony. They had technology back then, we just don't know what kind. Think of the pyramids, and Stonehenge, and other amazing feats by people without electricity or nuclear power. It was that or magic."

They all began to search for a way to open the door. They pushed on it, first on the left side, then the right, the top, the bottom, the centre. They looked for a button to press. The rock door did not budge.

"We have to get in there. Maybe we'll have to go down the lift after all," Fred said.

"And be ambushed in a cage?" Curtis snorted. "We don't know what might be waiting for us down there. The finfolk must be around here somewhere."

"Maybe they left the island," Cody suggested. "And left the prisoners where we couldn't get them."

They hadn't noticed that Kira was no longer with them. "Come in here!" she shouted from an adjoining room. "I need help to lift this stone." She was pulling on a metal handle attached to a large stone floor tile.

Fred could barely lift the stone alone. Once he had it partly up, Curtis and Cody lifted the edge and pushed until it fell open with a loud clatter. Below them, about three feet down, water swirled. When they looked inside, it appeared to be a tunnel carved from the rock, but even with their lamps they couldn't see where it went, or how deep it was.

"I'm going in," Kira said, giving Cody a sideways glance and short nod.

"Oh no, you're not." Fred had his hand on her shoulder and Curtis put his on her other shoulder. "It's far too dangerous. I promised your parents—"

"Yes, I know. But my other parents could be trapped inside the caverns. This might be a way to get into where they are. I just want to look. I can come back up if I need to."

"No, Kira, we'll find another way. Come on, let's close this up," Curtis said.

"Hey guys! Come here quick! The door in the wall is opening!" Cody hollered from the next room.

When Fred and Curtis ran off to see, Kira dove into the dark opening in the floor, into yet another tunnel. She smiled as she beat her tail and swam down, thinking what a great sidekick Cody was. They'd be annoyed with him for a while, but it would be worth it. They were on a mission, and she was the only one who could swim underwater.

Chapter Seventeen–
Banishing Dragons

Shortly after she dove in, the tunnel opened up. Kira could make out where the finfolk must have loaded the silver onto some sort of sledges that they could pull along the bottom and out into the open sea. It matched what they had seen from the cliff above. The water was still murky from recent disturbance of the sandy bottom, so she had to be careful in case any of them were still lurking about.

Kira turned back toward the island and explored the sides of the rock face for any openings. She moved back and forth, but found nothing. How far would she have to go to properly explore it and find another entrance, if there was one? She realized it could take days. Suddenly she didn't feel so clever anymore. She returned to the entrance of the tunnel and was about to turn into it when she noticed a movement on her left. She recognized the long grey face and pointy fin on the head of a finfolk heading straight for her.

Kira whipped her tail and shot up the tunnel as fast as she could. It wasn't far to the entrance in the smelter floor; she'd reach it before he could catch up to her. But when she had gone the distance that should have put her inside the building, she still hadn't reached it. She beat her tail harder, but the lamp on her head and the long gun strapped to her body slowed her down. She didn't dare look around; she had to stay as streamlined as possible. Also, the tunnel was getting smaller and tighter. What if she got wedged in or came to a dead end? The finfolk in pursuit was probably too large to get to her in a small space, but she could get stuck with no one to rescue her.

Then the tunnel widened a bit and, much relieved, Kira poured on the speed. Two beats later she came to a sudden stop, as if she'd hit an invisible wall. She found herself curled up, surrounded by a strong elastic web that was nearly transparent. Panic set in. She was trapped in a net! Kira tried to swim back the way she had come, but she was completely tangled. The net was wrapped around her arms, her head, her tail. As she thrashed around trying to push her way out, hearing only the pounding of her heart in her ears, she began to fear that she would never break free. No one would ever find her here, in a dead-end tunnel below the dungeons. Kira opened her mouth to scream when she heard a voice in her head.

"Kiiraaaa!" a man's voice echoed, from a long lost memory. She remembered strong arms thrusting her into a coarse net, a long beard that floated above her then disappeared, her name reverberating through the water. Then she envisioned the bright light that brought a gasp and cry from her mouth, and different arms scooping her out of the net. And in her memory she was free again.

Kira stopped struggling. She floated, still wrapped in netting, thinking about the distress of her dolphin friends when they were caught, sometimes by accident, sometimes by design. She wasn't going to be much use to them down here, trussed up like a sack of potatoes. She wasn't going to be much help to her parents and the other prisoners trapped in the dungeons.

Then she remembered how she had cut Cass loose. Slowly she inched her hand to her waist, and felt for the knife Cody had given her. It was there! She worked it out of its sheath, and carefully began to saw through the nylon netting, one strand at a time. Once her hand poked out she was able to work down along her tail, careful to keep the sharp edge pointed away from her body. Tail freed, then her other arm, then her head. She was out!

Did she dare to go back the way she came? In case the finfolk was waiting for her to go back, Kira decided to continue the way she'd been swimming, but more slowly now in case she ran into more netting. The tunnel widened slightly, then suddenly her head burst through to the surface. She gasped with relief. But she wasn't back where she'd started.

Quickly she flipped out of the water and examined the room she was in. Her headlamp was the only light in a wide, open cavern carved out of rock. The ceiling was rough and jagged and maybe three metres high.

As Kira's heart rate and breathing slowed, she began to hear faint erratic noises that were not the sounds of water. She crept forward, toward the sounds, sweeping her lamp over the ground and around her to be aware of anything or anyone who might try to surprise her.

As she followed the noises, she realized that they sounded much like voices, like people talking. Were they finfolk? Or the prisoners guarded by finfolk? Once or twice she stumbled on the uneven ground. She tried not to cry out when she stubbed her toe. No one needed to know she was coming until she knew who they were. Finally, she was able to make out individual voices. She switched off her headlamp and grabbed her gun.

"Did you see a light?"

"Yes, and finfolk don't use lights."

"Who is it? Who's out there?"

Kira did not answer. She had the sensation that someone nearby was watching her in the dark. She thought she heard a faint clicking sound on her right— like teeth tapping together. She swung around and pulled the trigger into the blackness.

"Aaaraaaghaa!" it screamed.

Kira switched on her headlamp, still holding the gun and ready to fire again. A finfolk was scampering away from her, still screaming. She swung her head all around and saw another one approaching her cautiously. She aimed her gun at him.

"I'll shoot!" she warned him. "The rest of our army is right behind me."

The reptilian monster glared at her and growled, but did not move. To Kira's surprise three more appeared and together they charged at her, snarling and snapping their jaws. She pulled the trigger, aiming at their mouths and their eyes, backing up as their momentum kept them moving toward her. Their roars were deafening. Her back was against the rock wall as she emptied her gun. The closest finfolk had dropped at her feet, writhing in agony, teeth still snapping inches from her. The others were crawling away back toward the water. Kira heard shouts amid the screams of the wounded finfolk. She moved along the wall to get away from the one still jerking on the ground, holding her empty gun in front of her in case he lunged at her. But he, too, finally slunk away and slipped into the water.

"Thank you, Cody," she muttered under her breath. "The lemon juice worked, you're a genius."

Amid all the shouting she heard a voice call out, "Kira? Is that you?" It was Calista. From the dark, people materialized in front of her, and the crowd continued to grow. Their echoing voices in the cavern grew into thunder until she couldn't understand what anyone was saying. She was hugged, kissed, and hugged again, over and over.

Finally Currin called for quiet. The noise slowly subsided, although a few children whimpered quietly at the back of the crowd.

"Kira, I don't know how you found us, yet again, or what you did to those bullies, but we thank you from the bottom of our hearts."

Kira blushed in the darkness, her heart thundering in her chest. She may have found them, but how were they going to get out of the cavern? They couldn't swim via the tunnel. Currin answered her unspoken question.

"And now those monsters are gone, we can leave this most dreadful prison."

Kira followed him and the others to another large cavern.

"Kira, we need to find the door into the smelter," Currin said. "Shine your lamp over these walls, it should be nearby. Aha! Here it is!"

As she illuminated what looked like a featureless wall, she watched Currin poke at it in several places, as if he was punching in a code. The wall seemed to groan, and then a round crack appeared and the door began to move in and roll to one side.

"Mothers and children first," someone instructed after a couple of men first checked that it was safe on the other side. Kira saw that Calista had Amelie and Borin with her when they stepped through the opening into the smelter. When nearly everyone had passed through, she heard a familiar voice on the other side.

"Kira! I told them the door was opening and they didn't believe me." She stepped through to find Cody standing there, a huge shiny grin on his face. For a moment, she thought of the metal-coated teeth of the finfolk, and she began to laugh. They each raised their right arms for a celebratory high five. Then her mother, Bess, was hugging her tight, trying not to cry. Kira grinned, but felt near tears herself.

Outside the smelter was mayhem. People greeting each other, crying, laughing, and most gratifying of all, reuniting with family. Curtis discovered that his uncle was amongst the prisoners, a merrow whom the family believed had died over thirty years ago. They also found Charles Graham, the youngest brother of Marcus, who had loaned his boat *Saving Grace* to the expedition. His other brother had perished in the attack on their fishing vessel.

Once all the connections had been made, Curtis and Fred began to arrange information meetings for the adults to organize their passage back home. It would

Orysia Dawydiak

require several boat trips to take that many people. The crowds gradually thinned as those who lived in Digger's Hill returned to their homes and the rest had a longer walk back to Noville. Though the finfolk appeared to be gone, the villagers walked back in large groups in case any had been left behind. Calista invited Kira, Cody, and Bess to come back with them to have a meal. They all agreed they were starving after the ordeal, rescuers and captives alike.

Neither Borin nor Amelie spoke to Kira on their way back to the village. Kira didn't mind. She had the satisfaction of having accomplished what she had set out to do. But she wouldn't be fully content until they were all off that horrible island.

Up ahead of her she heard Cody explaining to Fred and Curtis how the lemon juice worked against finfolk. "You see, lemon juice is highly acidic. If it gets in your eyes it burns, right? Well it turns out that the facial skin of finfolk has a chemistry that is super sensitive and porous to acid, especially ascorbic acid. It's absorbed into the body tissues so it feels like they're on fire from the inside out. Nasty, but effective."

"But how did you know that?" Fred asked.

"I spent a lot of time at the library researching it. In the stories I read about them, certain things kept coming up in battles with their enemies. So I checked the sources, followed up references, just normal research protocol. And I came up with a hypothesis. Luckily it worked."

Kira saw Fred and Curtis look at each other and shake their heads. Cody was probably not going to be a fisherman when he grew up, or a dentist like his father. Kira was so proud of her geeky friend.

At the highest point on their walk back someone shouted and everyone froze. "It's gone! The fog ring is gone!" A cheer rose up like a wave starting at the top of the hill and flowing down from person to person along the path. People clapped, jumped up and down, and cried.

"I imagine that's the first time the fog has lifted since the finfolk took it over," Curtis said. "I do believe they have truly left. Let's hope it's for good."

Once they reached Noville and began to make plans, Kira realized that many of the rescued people had no homes to go to off the island. The older merrows had not only lost their underwater homes, but also the ability to change back into their undersea forms. They would have a lot of adjustments to make once they reached the mainland. She was also surprised to hear that about a hundred of the inhabitants had decided to stay now the finfolk were gone. They were born on Hildaland and considered it home. Curtis promised to leave behind the lemon juice shooters in case any finfolk decided to reclaim the island. And a couple of dories so they could finally fish for themselves.

Kira wondered if Borin and Amelie were hoping to return to their underwater home and to their parents. If they still had a home to return to. At that moment she pitied them, thinking they might never see their parents again. She wondered if they would ever accept that their mother was a finfolk.

Kira looked forward to finally be leaving Hildaland behind. She was anxious to find her dolphin friends, to learn if they were okay. Besides the bodies of several sharks, whales, and even a couple of reptilian finfolk on the beach, there did not seem to be any live sentries patrolling the waters. After supper and as soon as Kira was aboard a dory to return to the ship for the night, she leaned over, stuck her head underwater, and called. Cass popped up shortly and gave her a report. He was one of three dolphins who had disobeyed orders and gone through the fog ring. One of his friends had an injured flipper, but was going to recover, he said.

"And Sherman?" Kira asked. He was the main reason their boats had been saved from sinking. He was probably responsible for all the casualties on the beach.

"Sherman is in great form," Cass said. "And so are his two brothers, Max and Cesar. Even giant octopuses need backup sometimes. They were having so much fun, they went off to chase the finfolk. We didn't follow, we're in enough trouble already."

Kira smiled at Cass's impish expression. "Will you be okay? With your dad?"

"Sure, don't worry about me. That was the most fun I've had since...I don't know when. Anyway, remember to call if you decide to have any more adventures, Princess Kira. Must be off now. Your path is clear to home. The rest of those spineless sharks and whales took off once they saw Sherman and company in action." With that he squeaked, leaped out of the water, and disappeared under the dory in a burst of bubbles.

Once they were on the boats again the next day and heading for home, Kira relaxed. Each boat took as many passengers as was safe, about 150 altogether. All four of her parents were on board *Saving Grace*, something Kira had never imagined happening. Cody was giving Borin and Amelie a tour and talking their ears off. Her father was explaining the navigational equipment to Currin and Charles Graham. Bess was speaking earnestly with Calista on the deck.

The two women finally approached Kira, both smiling, though her mother wore her worried expression. She said, "Calista and Currin and your cousins will be staying with the MacDonalds in town while they sort things out. You know, look for work, get the kids settled in school and such. Once they have a place of their own, we thought we'd let you decide where you wanted to live. I mean, they are your actual parents. And you went to a lot of trouble to find them. And it's good you did." She sniffed and looked away for a moment.

It had never occurred to Kira that she would live anywhere but with her adoptive parents. She cared for Calista and Currin, but they were more like an aunt and uncle to her. And then there were her cousins. Maybe they'd become friends one day, but she was quite happy to remain an only child.

"Oh Mom, and Calista, it's nice of you to give me a choice, but I think I'd better stay where I am. You and Currin will be busy enough, especially with those two." She nodded in the direction of her cousins. Amelie was now talking Cody's ear off.

Calista gave Kira a long hug. "You are a wise one, so grown up and yet so young. I am proud that you are my daughter, a true princess. A brave and selfless princess."

Bess blinked away her tears and stroked Kira's hair. "Yes, she is growing up fast, and has a mind of her own. But once we're back home, Miss Kira, you can forget about the princess thing. You've no idea how all your escapades have aged me these past months."

"Yes I do," Kira laughed. "Your red hair is turning pink from all the white hair I've given you. Sorry, Mom." She gave her mother a quick hug, then ran off to save Cody from her jabbering cousins.

The small fleet of seven ships sailed through the night toward the families and friends who awaited them on the mainland. Kira lay awake in her berth, in the dark. She was exhausted, but too agitated to sleep. The thought of Mrs. Doyle being reunited with her husband after such a long time made her feel especially good, even thrilled. But her parents and so many other merrows would never be able to return to their original homes. And if Merhaven was lost completely to the finfolk, what had become of all the merrows who had lived there?

Kira squeezed her eyes shut and tried not to think about them, about merrows like the kind, elderly servant who had helped her escape Merhaven. It should be enough that she had found her parents, and now they were free. And yet, she was not satisfied. Merhaven was her ancestral home, and it should be returned to the merrow race. And just how was a thirteen-year-old mermaid going to make that happen?

She would have to sleep on it. Maybe her dreams would reveal the way.

Acknowledgements

Many thanks to my wise and thoughtful
editors, Penelope Jackson and Laurie Brinklow.
I am also grateful to Kira's fans, from nine to ninety,
who have waited patiently for her latest exploits.
And finally, to my fabulous WWW writing group—I
am so fortunate to be part of your wave, crossing
uncharted seas to novel shores.